Sophie Drake and the Smoking Man

Sophie Drake Mysteries #2

Anne Shelley

PUBLISHING

MARTIN IN THE WOODS PUBLISHER

To Richard Mueller who inspires and encourages, a true wordsmith whose dedication to the craft and generosity of spirit have helped me write not just this book but many others.

Contents

Where I get a Rude Awakening

Sometimes I feel I am not moving in time but just falling forward repeatedly to whatever fate has already decided is next for me.

In this case, next was a burned-out smoke shop. Where ironically a hundred thousand dollars' worth of cigarettes had just burned to ash.

This was the third fire in a row for the arsonist, and the most interesting one so far.

***

The first I heard of the case was a call from Harry after the second building burned. "Got a job for you. Come into the office at twelve," Harry grunted and hung up, not waiting for hello or goodbye. If he'd been slightly younger he would have texted me but that wasn't Harry's style. It was eleven. I should probably be up. May as well go in. I dragged myself out of bed and stepped over the pile of clothes that lay on the floor. I'd deal with that later. I remembered why my clothes were thrown around and looked about. I was alone. Well, at least there was that to be thankful for.

I put on some meditation music and hopped in the shower. I was never really going to meditate but at least listening to the music might make me calmer, right? I couldn't believe I'd broken my vow. I was pissed at myself. I would have to deal with the consequences tomorrow. For today, Harry had a job for me. I hadn't been working enough lately. That was the real problem. Harry hadn't been hustling for jobs since he'd gotten the big payout from Daddy Butterworth in July.

The man paid us more in hush money than he would have ever paid us to actually find his daughter, so those funds had given Harry a bigger nest egg than he'd ever had. He actually talked for two minutes about closing the company, then he'd realized that would give him more time at home with his momma and he'd been back at the office twelve hours a day. Still, it had been almost a month since I'd had a job. That was the real problem, I thought, noticing the pile of wet towels in the corner of the room. Couldn't anyone put anything in the hamper? Living alone rarely gives me the opportunity to blame others for the mess but this time there was someone to blame. I shouldn't have done it. Yes, it had been too long since I'd worked, and idleness is the devil's plaything.

Thinking of the devil, I tried to scrub all the memories of the night before off, the good and the bad—oh so bad, in such a good way. What the hell was wrong with me? I couldn't even keep a promise to myself? I would keep my vow. At least I would keep my vow from now on.

By the time I got to the office I had properly castigated myself, had most of the sleep rubbed out of my eyes and, more importantly, I'd downed half of a triple-shot latte, so I was pretty much as human as I was going to get. I walked out of the bright sunlit day into the office and almost hit the walker our new client had parked by the door.

"Mrs. Arkbari, this is my associate Sophie Drake. She'll be the one out in the field investigating your case."

I looked down at my watch. I was only fifteen minutes late, but the meeting had already been going on a while by the unsigned contract in front of Mrs. Arkbari.

Mrs. Arkbari turned to stare at me with obsidian eyes that cut right through me. She judged me instantly and found me lacking. She knew everything I had ever done and she was ashamed for me, and of me. Her eyes had seen all there was to see and were too damaged to close again. I guessed by looking at her that she was somewhere between 70 and 200 years old. Her face was still strong and proud but her body was disappearing, slowly dissolving away, getting thinner and thinner till there would be nothing left. Her hair had lost its color and had been replaced by a long silver mane that still shone in the sunlight from the window.

"Nice to meet you," I said, waving the way one does since the pandemic. Her twisted knuckles and veins sitting in the lap did not move. I leaned against my desk—standing up, facing them—put down the coffee and prepared to hear the story.

Mrs. Arkbari turned to Harry. "She looks so young. Don't you have anyone else?"

Harry smiled the large crocodile smile he only gets when he is getting annoyed. "I will put my best people on your job. And Sophie is the best of the best." He slid his eyes sideways at me. "And she is older than she looks. Now if you don't mind, I'll have you repeat your case rather than me reading my notes to her. It will also give me the opportunity to write more notes in case you add something you didn't already tell me."

The old woman turned to Harry and nodded. She'd been brought up in a time and culture when you followed all instructions from men and wasn't about to argue, despite her lack of trust in my abilities.

"My family left Iran in 1979, escaping the Revolution. We came to Los Angeles and my father started investing in real estate. Over the years we reinvested most of the profits from his other business into more real estate. Anyway, at this point I own approximately three hundred properties in Los Angeles."

"Three hundred," I said, shocked, repeating the number so my brain could process. Three hundred properties. In Los Angeles. Wow. In a city where a condo could easily cost a million dollars, that was quite a bit of investment.

"Yes," she said, obviously accustomed to getting this reaction. "Mostly small apartment buildings and small commercial properties, strip malls, etc."

"And she's just had two different properties she owns burned to the ground," said Harry, motioning me to shut my mouth with his hand, so I guess my jaw was still hanging open. I mean, I've thought about what stinking-rich people would look like, and somehow elegantly withered women never fell into my list of possible profiles.

"Yes, both of my properties in East Hollywood were damaged—an apartment building on Virgil and a strip mall on Vermont. The fire department says it's definitely arson."

"Sophie, I am putting you on this full-time until you find the person responsible."

I groaned inwardly. If someone really was torching her buildings, then it was probably someone she knew. Someone who hated her. Unless it was just random and unlucky. Either way, this wasn't going to be fun.

I pulled a pad of paper and a pen out of my desk, pulled a seat up closer to her, and sat down. "Ok, so do you own any other properties in the area?"

"Just those two."

"Were there any other arson attempts on any other properties in the area?"

"I don't know."

"Do you know anyone who would like to hurt you, or who may be angry with you about anything? "

"What are you insinuating, young woman?"

"Well, either there is a firebug who is hitting properties randomly in Hollywood and you just got unlucky that two were yours, or someone knows your property holdings and is targeting you personally. If that's the case, it's probably someone you know and this is probably an attack on you."

"Oh..." She looked a little stunned. It was obvious she'd never thought that this could actually be personal. "Well, yes, I see..."

"I will check with the fire department to see if this is some kind of coincidence and there were other fires in the area, but could you sit down and make a list of people you know who might be angry enough to do something like this?"

"There is no one."

"Please think about it at home and get back to me."

"Well, if you think I have to, I can have my assistant work on it."

"If I can get your assistant's name and phone number I will talk to them directly."

She pulled out a card and handed it over to me. It was a beautiful card, thick, with gold writing on a matt black background. "If you call the office number Maria will pick up. She's my assistant."

"Thank you," I said, looking down at the piece of card that belonged to an earlier time and a different culture than the one I lived in. I vaguely remembered my dad having a collection of these, but I had never seen one as pretty as this.

"Thank you so much for coming in," said Harry, standing up. He walked around to her side of the desk. "We will be in touch shortly with more questions and if we discover anything. If you can have your assistant send back the contract after your lawyer reviews it and you have signed it, we will begin work right away."

"Thank you, sir," she said, almost as if Harry was her better, which of course, he most definitely was not. She'd been taught to treat men as people superior to her and by the way she was looking at me as she turned she thought most women, or at least I, were completely beneath her. Which I probably—no, most definitely—was.

I had taken the job with Harry because, quite frankly, I'd looked for a job for so long and he was the only one who was offering to hire me.

I hadn't seen him in years, not since my dad's funeral. My mom had reached out to him and told him I needed work. He'd agreed to meet with Barry's kid.

He sat there at the restaurant where he'd agreed to meet me, his eyes darting about, not at ease, not at all comfortable sitting with a female in a restaurant.

I looked out. I'd seen him arrive. I'd arrived before he had and saw him drive up in his ancient green Porsche. So I figured he had enough money to pay my salary. We sat down across from each other. Like combatants do, or people in a police interrogation.

And he ordered himself a beer. Something I am pretty sure wouldn't be approved in any guidelines on hiring.

I decided to drink nothing but water. The job interview was long. Not as long as some, but long enough for him to eat a salad and spill half of it down his shirt. At 65 or so, Harry hadn't seemed to work out the social graces that everyone else considered normal. Whether it was eating (he let his mouth shut and open intermittently while chewing, or not), drinking beer during a job interview or just everything Harry touched. He just did things a little bit differently, but then when he started to talk, you could see how smart he was underneath. The external frame that was his body—that wasn't him. His mind was brilliant.

He'd started off as a detective at the LAPD. He'd known my dad. He must have started with the force a hundred years back. When they still rode horses. Well, maybe not quite that long, but almost. And now he had a detective agency in Los Angeles. It was famous enough that it got celebrity clients. And discreet enough that it kept them.

Harry was not a man to be messed with. You could tell that by the tattoos and his still bulky arms. The tattoo on his forearm wasn't a fun modern tribal design. It said he had been a paratrooper. Which war? You didn't want to ask.

I stood and she stood too, pulling herself up unobtrusively with the table. She was taller than me by a little. When she was younger she would have been at least five foot four inches. She still carried herself straight and would have been a beautiful woman in her youth. She'd never had any work done, or if she had it had been done so well that her strong features still seemed individual and unique. Hers was not an easy face but it was the face of a woman who had survived.

Harry brought her walker to her and helped her to the door, and I followed. She walked out and got into a newer Toyota, nothing that denoted her wealth, and drove herself out of the lot.

"So, Harry, what did she tell you?"

"If you'd gotten here faster you would have heard most of it."

"If I'd gotten here faster I wouldn't ask. So don't be angry. I already have a headache. Just tell me what you know." We walked back inside and Harry pulled out his notes. "First fire was eight days ago. The apartment building she owns on Virgil went up. Fire two was last night. That's when she reached out to me.

"This time the fire was at night. In a strip mall on Vermont and Fountain. The fire started in the laundromat but no one was hurt."

"Ok," I said. "Could just be a coincidence."

"But it's not," responded Harry, "and you are meeting with the arson investigator to see what else you can find."

"Ok," I said. How bad could meeting a fireman be? I was hoping he looked like one in the calendars.

Fireman Fantasies and Flamed-out Washers

I arrived at the burned-out apartment on Virgil and parked a block away, in what was a mostly legal parking spot on the street. The apartment building was on the corner of Virgil and DeLongpre. Both busy city streets with more cop cars passing than pedestrians. It had a lovely view of the thirty or so cars and decrepit motorhomes which were parked behind the graffitied dumpsters of the local supermarket. A neighborhood of the homeless.

I walked over to the site, the smell of exhaust and human urine in my nose. I knew they didn't want me on the site alone, so the fire department was having the arson specialist meet me. I walked up. I don't know what I'd been expecting. Maybe a guy... you know, in full fire gear with a big fire hat. And full-on fire equipment.

But Jeff Delmonico was standing there in a blue polo and uniform pants that worked really well with his rear. On his head was a hard hat and he had one in his hand, obviously to give me.

I walked up.

"Hello. I'm Sophie Drake. I think you're expecting me."

"Yes," he said, obviously less than impressed that he had to do this.

"Do I have to wear this?" I said, pointing to the hard hat.

He looked at me, holding the hat out with a mild look of disgust. "Yeah, we have to. The building is burned out. The structure is unstable. Things, like the ceiling, could fall."

"Ok," I said, only mildly terrified. I put it on and he unlocked the temporary fences around the scene of the fire. We walked in between the frame of the building and the space where once there had been a fence gate. All around us were the pieces that had fallen away. Shattered windows, doors that had burst open from the inside, allowing the flame to lick its way up the wall and onto the roof.

It had been a three-story building—garage below, and two stories of apartments above. It had been built like a U with all the apartments reached by outside balconies looking down on the driveway. On the stairs was a pink radio flyer tricycle, its wheels bent and its tires melted into a stain on the step.

You could see that people had lived here and that they had left in a hurry. Or maybe they had died trying to get out. I hadn't thought to ask. I hadn't thought what a fire did to an apartment building. To the lives of the people that lived there. To all they had and all they treasured.

He led me to the center of the driveway where all the tenants would have driven in with their cars. This was where the kids would have played, the safest place to be on a street as busy as this one. I could see the remains of chalk paintings on the concrete. Lying on the ground, a pair of plain white women's underwear, cotton, from someone larger than me, dirty and covered in ash. A chest of drawers had been thrown out of an apartment and shattered. It had obviously been ransacked by a homeless person. All the smoke-filled clothes were scattered about the ground. And then a skateboard with nothing left. The board on the top charred. The wheels melted off. Almost nothing had dissolved to ash. More like everything had been transformed into something else. Horrifying and deeply sad.

I followed Jeff closely, checking out his ass. He was about as handsome and as well built as firemen usually are in my fantasies. And I was not unhappy to have met him, no matter how dismissive he was being of me.

"Where did the fire start, Jeff?"

He turned around to look at me. "I'm taking you there." We walked down two or three stairs to a small room that was in the corner of the garage. It was a laundry room. There was nothing but black. The metal of the washers was black. The walls black, black holes up into the apartment above us. Like the night had come and invaded the room.

"The fire started here in the washing machine. Whoever lit it, they knew what they were doing. The fire went straight up there."

He pointed to the black trails that had been wiring. "The fire followed the wiring up into the building. Straight up through the roof. This was a perfect spot to start it because it's almost in the center of the building. And because they would have been pretty much unobserved. And the laundry room was never locked. Anybody could have gotten in here to do it."

I looked at the remains of the coin-operated washing machines, the coin slots melted and twisted in the heat. "Ok. And you're sure this was arson?"

"Oh yes. Look up there. See this? This area was covered in propellant. It burned very, very hot. We've tested the residue and not only was it arson, it was a very specific arsonist because they used airplane fuel as the accelerant."

"Airplane fuel?"

"Yeah, really high-grade gasoline that contains lead. It's for small aircraft. It's not something you can just buy at the corner store. Avgas 100LL. We believe that the entire area was covered in airplane fuel and the fire was probably contained in this room with the door shut for about 5 minutes before it exploded up into the rest of the building."

I thought I better ask the question I'd been wanting to ask since I first saw the tricycle. "I wondered about the inhabitants of the building. Did they all get out?"

"Yeah, all of the inhabitants of the building were actually able to leave. The fire was lit during the daytime. Most of them were at work."

I wondered where they were living now. It wasn't like it was easy to find a cheap apartment in Los Angeles. And by the looks of this place, it had been a cheap apartment. Had always been a cheap apartment. And it was under rent control because it was old. A rent-controlled apartment. If you moved in a few years ago, you might only be paying twelve, thirteen hundred bucks. Now that same amount of money wouldn't get you in a bedroom in a shared house in the suburbs.

"Do you have any more questions, miss?"

"No, no, thank you. I believe the other property in question is just up the road."

Jeff turned around and looked at me for the first time, really looking at me. From my head down to my toes, back to my head, and then settled his eyes firmly on my boobs. There is almost nothing as unattractive as being given the once-up-and-down by a man. All of a sudden, he went from being my hot fireman fantasy to being just another creep who'd just noticed I was a woman. The fact that I had been objectifying him and checking out his butt for at least ten minutes in no way made him less distasteful.

"Yeah, the other property is just, like, two blocks across. I can take you there. We can just get my car. I'm parked right here." He was leading me out and locking the temporary fences. I noticed his car was parked in front of the fire hydrant. I suppose that was one of the perks of actually being a fireman. And it wasn't like anyone needed to use the hydrant. Everything that could burn had burnt. Even the palm trees in front had turned into large leafless toothpicks pointed to the sky.

I looked down at my car a half a block away and hopped into the red fire vehicle's empty passenger seat. We drove down and I filled the silence with questions. "So what was the next property that burned?" I said, asking what I knew already.

"It was in this strip mall," he said, pointing to our left to the corner of Lexington and Vermont. "The fire was started in the laundromat."

"It was a self-service laundromat," I said, looking at the signs above the burned-out, boarded-up business. "So not the same MO."

"Exactly. Normally firebugs like to burn the same kind of building," Jeff said as he pulled the car into the strip mall parking lot. "But it was confirmed this morning that the same propellant was used. So we know it's the same firebug."

"Ok."

He drove up in front of the boarded-up coin-operated laundry. Next door was a pet store, which was still surprisingly full of stock and had live fish swimming in tanks at the window. And on the other side was a tobacco store. And next to that was a mailbox place. The arsonist had picked the middle store in the strip mall, and the biggest one. It was just surprising that the entire strip mall hadn't gone up—only that one shop.

The store was set back into the corner. Jeff went and unlocked the door, and the smell hit me. Unlike the apartment building where the doors had been blown open and the windows shattered, the laundromat had been boarded up and somehow the smell of the burning, the rubber, the metal, the heat, the propellant had all been trapped inside the building.

"Where did this one start?" I said to Jeff, not wanting to walk further into the building.

"Two dryers at the back. Looks like they were filled with towels that were soaked in airplane fuel. Set on a high heat and then the perpetrator walked out."

"Ok. Do we have any video of who was using the dryer?"

"No, no. It was late in the evening. All the other businesses were closed. They all have internal cameras.""The laundry didn't have cameras?"

"Sure, they have internal cameras here too. But the heat was such that it melted the camera, it melted the DVR, melted the whole system. They didn't have it attached to any external recording device or any cloud storage, so we don't have any record of the person."

"Was anyone hurt?"

"No, no. Apparently the perpetrator was careful to make sure that the place was empty. Now we do suspect that they, you know, picked the center of the building because they wanted the entire place to go up. But it turned out that there was actually an employee on duty. She was just using the lavatory, which is down at the end of the strip mall, and when she came back out of the lavatory, she saw the smoke and called 911."

"This building didn't burn as fast?""No. Because it's a commercial building, it had a slower burn time. And the fire station is just down the road. They were able to get here before the pet shop went up, and the animals were ok. And none of the other stores were burned. Don't get me wrong, there was smoke damage and, you know, most of these businesses won't actually be open again for some time, but the only thing that needs to be completely rebuilt, of course, is the laundromat."

I looked around at the charcoal remains of more coin-operated washers and dryers, just like at the first fire but the machines bigger this time. More of them. It seemed weird to me that both of the fires had started in laundries. Maybe it was just a coincidence.

"So you've seen enough?"

"Yeah. Thank you."

"Let me give you a ride back to your car."

"Oh, it's ok. I'll just walk back. I've got a lot to think about."

"Oh, no, no, no bother. I'll take you." It was easier to say yes than no. I got back in the car.

"So how long have you been a detective?" he asked. His job was over. He'd shown me everything that had already happened. But I needed to think—about why it had happened and about what could happen next. I didn't want to be quizzed. But I answered.

"About a year."

"Oh, so you're just new to this?" he said.

"Actually, I used to be a police detective before this."

"Cute little thing like you was a police detective?"

Any hotness had just worn off my fireman fantasy. Jeff had done it. Those cute little curls coming out underneath his hard hat were not enough.

"So how long have you been a fireman?" I said.

"Oh, I'm not just a fireman, love. I'm an arson investigator. I've been an arson investigator for five years."

"Oh, five years as an arson investigator? Well, so sorry you haven't advanced. I would have thought you could have, you know, been a fire chief or something in five years."

He decided that I was being stupid rather than dismissive and condescending. "No, no, you don't understand. Being an arson investigator is a really high position. It's a really skilled job."

"Oh yeah, cute little things like me, we don't always get it." The rest of the drive back to the car was silent.

Let's not Rule out Terrorists

I opened my email the next morning. Mrs. Arkbari's assistant, Maria, had filled out my questionnaire. In all fairness, she'd tried to answer the questions with full answers, tried to give me as much information as she could, but it was pretty much useless.

Mrs. Arkbari didn't seem to believe that she could possibly be the target of these attacks, although she most obviously was. I groaned reading the list. The question was, "People who might want to hurt the business or the principal." The list said, "terrorists, and extremists." This was going to need some more leg work.

I groaned. There were no terrorists that I had ever heard of that target rich old ladies by burning their assets. Whoever had done this either knew her personally and knew what she owned, or had just accidentally burned two properties with the same owner. I realized I would actually have to talk to the fire department again. And what's worse, I would have to call and talk to the arson investigator. I pulled up my notes on my phone. I couldn't remember his name. The guy I had pissed off and alienated was Jeff Delmonico.

I should learn from this experience and stop pissing off strangers who might be useful to me. On the other hand, how do you measure someone's usefulness before you say something that is both witty and accurate, and guaranteed to offend? If only I could keep my mouth closed. But that is not really one of my life skills. I should see if the UCLA has a class in keeping your fucking mouth shut. But the more awkward the situation, the cuter the guy, the more chance that I will completely blow it.

I called the station and they put me through to him. His voice dropped as I introduced myself. His hello went down at least half in tone and volume. "Yes."

Sometimes yes is the most awful word. This was definitely one of those times. I decided to make it short for both of us. Pleasantries were for people I hadn't pissed off yet.

"I was just wondering if there were any other fires that used the same propellant?"

"No."

"Thank you." I hung up. I had nothing left to say.

Two fires and they both just happened to be properties owned by the same person. It could be bad luck but probably not. Seemed about as probable as me waking up tomorrow morning and finding out I was a princess.

So I called Mrs. Arkbari's office number. Her assistant, Maria, one of those efficient-sounding women, picked up. I was sure 90 percent of her job was probably stopping sales calls, so I wanted her to know asap that I was not selling a security system or advertising. "Hi. This is Sophie Drake. I work for HR Security. I am investigating the arson of your two properties."

"Hi, Sophie. I am Maria. I sent you the information this morning."

"Fabulous," I said, doing the normal thing now that I did on the phone. I put her on speaker and walked outside where I could feel the sun on my head and watch the squirrels and try to drive the bad taste out of my mouth that Mr. Fire Arson Investigator had left.

"Maria, can I level with you?"

"Yes," she said in a way that was completely different from the yes I got earlier from the man. It was a yes that said 'I already understand what you are going to say. I have seen things and I am here to help you. We are in this together, girl.'

"Maria, the paperwork you sent me earlier... it wasn't particularly helpful."

"It was what Mrs. Arkbari wanted me to write."

"I understand no one wants to think that they could have personal enemies but the nature of these fires leads me to believe that the person who committed the crimes knows not only your boss but also what assets she owns. I was hoping you could provide me with a list of anyone who you think either has an issue with Mrs. A and—or—has the details of what real estate she owns."

"Real estate is a matter of public record."

"Does she hold all her real estate in her name?"

"No, they are held in trusts. Both of these properties were in the same trust. She only has two different trusts. One owns the properties bought before she took over in 1989 and one for properties bought after."

"Which trust owned these properties?"

"The one set up by her father pre-1989. I will send you the details. And you need to realize that there are four different companies that are contracted to us to maintain the properties."

"These properties were in the same area. Were they maintained by the same company?" I picked a stick up out of the parking area and threw it under a bush. *Please, please say yes*, I thought. Right now there were about ten million people in the city and the only people I was sure were innocent were me, Mrs. A and Harry. And maybe the guy I slept with the other night... what was his name?

"Yes, they are maintained by the same company. Bronson Construction."

"How many properties do they maintain?" I asked, silently hoping it was less than ten.

"They maintain everything in Hollywood and Downtown, so approximately seventy," Maria answered. "I can give you their number. The person I work with is Amanda. I can tell her to expect a call."

"That's amazing, Maria, but could you let her know I would like to come by and speak with her? And since this is all going to be far more intensive than I was hoping, I would love to come talk face to face with you too. Could I come by this afternoon?"

The one thing I have noticed since COVID is that seeing people in person is even more illuminating than ever. Just seeing humans is somehow unsettling. And if Maria had anything to hide, I would definitely know face to face.

"Sounds great," said Maria and I was already sure she wasn't trying to hide anything, because she wanted me to visit. I made the appointment for two hours' time and I went to grab a burrito at Chipotle before I put a call into Amanda at Bronson Construction.

Amanda was the kind of hard woman who ends up working in an industry dominated by men. She answered the phone with a low grumble and it seemed like every word I said was a huge inconvenience to her life. I was quite obviously wasting her time and energy, and was the kind of imposition that had to be tolerated to pass the day and get a paycheck.

I was wondering if we could meet maybe this afternoon?" I said.

"I work till three."

Not a yes or a no, more of a distraction from my question. "I could be there at 1 p.m."

"I take my lunch at 1 p.m."

"Ok, then I will be there at 2 p.m."

"I eat my lunch at my desk."

Wow. So she was there all day. And she couldn't say that.

"Ok. I will be there ASAP. Could I bring you a coffee?"

"Venti skinny sugar-free vanilla latte iced, with an extra shot and cold foam cream."

Well, the only thing that was going to be good about this day was that I could legitimately expense my coffee run.

Queen Bee and her Kingdom of Paper

I n person, Amanda was much as I had imagined her on the phone. With carefully streaked blonde hair and a thin face with a nose someone had paid to get fixed when she was a much younger person. Her figure was rounding out as women do post-menopause, but her lips were as thin and judgmental as they had ever been. She was a woman unhappy about where her life had led her, and now she sat as the queen of her office, papers neatly stacked and pens lined in a row in a drawer. She reminded me vaguely of my tenth-grade teacher, the one we all bet had never been laid.

"Hi, Amanda. I'm Sophie Drake. We spoke on the phone." She turned and looked over her two computer monitors at me and motioned me to give her the coffee.

I handed it over and pulled up a chair and sat.

"Yes. What can I do for you?"

"I am sure you heard that two of Mrs. Arkbari's properties were destroyed and I am working for Mrs. Arkbari to investigate the fires.

How long has your company been doing maintenance for Mrs. Ark-bari?"

"Since March 20th, 1997."

"Wow, that's a long time. I'm sure you weren't here then. Probably still in school?" I was trying to be sweet; it's not something I do very well.

"Actually, no, I was here."

Holy shit, her life really had been pretty fucked. Who the hell stayed at the same job for that long? Maybe she was part-owner? God, I hoped she was. Now how to word this in case she wasn't.

"So has there been any change in ownership of the company recently?"

"No. Mr. Bronson started the company in 1993 and he's the sole owner."

I looked at her cheap Staples desk and her well-worn budget office chair where her widening behind had pushed most of the foam sideways. I was pretty sure this hadn't been her dream when she left school.

"Ok, so how many employees do you have working on Mrs. Ark-bari's properties?"

"We have a crew of seventeen, but much of the work we do for her is done by our subcontractors."

I'd been thinking seventeen... I can investigate seventeen people; that's not so hard. But subcontractors? "How many subcontractors do you use?"

"Well, it depends on the area and the problem. We have plumbing subcontractors, and electrical, and roofing, and we've had the window guys there, and—"

"How many subcontractors do you do business with?"

"We've got about eighty that we go to, depending upon the need."

"Eighty?" *Fuck me*, I thought. "And those eighty are individuals?"

"Oh no, they are mostly companies. Like, Johnson Plumbing I think has about three hundred employees."

I groaned audibly. "Are you ok?" She stared her beady eyes down her ski-lift nose at me. It wasn't a question of concern but of judgement. "You don't sound well."

For a moment I got a flash of Amanda at high school. She would have been popular, one of those popular blonde mean girls that everyone wants to be. The kind of girl who makes life hell for other girls while at the same time being the one all the boys want.

"I am fine, thank you." I would need to sigh internally from now on. "Would you have a record of who worked on the two properties in question in the last year or so?"

"Of course. I don't know why Mrs. Arkbari couldn't provide that to you. It's not like we don't give her copies of all the invoices."

"If I could get a copy from you, that would be great," I said.

"I don't have time to pull out just the files on those properties. We file all the information for her together." Amanda flashed a mean smile at me, showing the perfect little teeth that had probably all been capped by now. "I have this box of files just from her properties for the last two months. Further back there are other boxes."

I remembered when I'd been on the force they'd had a file room filled with file cabinets, and I'd wondered when the days of paperless offices were ever going to come to pass, but at least we'd had file cabinets. All this woman had in her disappointing life was a storeroom filled with bankers' boxes filled with papers.

"Could I look at them?" I asked.

"Yes, but the papers do not leave my office. You can look over there." She pointed to a sad-looking glass dining table which was pretending to be a conference table. "Do not take any papers out. If you need to copy them, I have a copier but you will need to pay me for the copies."

"Ok." I nodded, planning to take photos of anything that actually interested me. The boxes were marked with the addresses of the properties and the dates. She had all boxes for the current month piled up by her desk, and I took the right one to the table.

I got to the table and opened the box. It was well organized, all things considered, by week, and then inside each folder of weekly service orders and accounting receipts the properties themselves were filed in numerical order by street number. Amanda might not be a sweet little thing anymore but she was competent at her job and her paperwork was in order. I wished I could say the same. It was time to get my taxes ready and at the rate things were going I'd have to file an extension again.

Now that I'd worked out her system it was pretty easy to see what had been done at the two different addresses.

The laundromat and apartment building had both had service calls from the same plumber and from the same electrician. So just a few hundred people... and the local construction crew, which appeared to work directly as part of Bronson Construction—at least some of their seventeen employees—had also been out.

I snapped pictures of the invoices for the plumber and electrician. I would need to talk to them next. This was going to be such a very, very long week. I walked the box back to Amanda.

In the time it had taken me to look at a couple of files she had snorted down the coffee like a coke addict out on parole.

"Thank you so much. Your files are so well organized I was able to do that so easily."

She blushed slightly and gave a genuine smile. Then shut that down. She reopened the box to make sure I hadn't messed up her files. "So are you done now?"

"Could I see the rest of the boxes for this year?" She nodded, stood and walked me back to the rear of the office where she opened the door and switched on the light. There in the windowless storeroom were wall-to-ceiling boxes of paperwork. She pointed to the shelf on the far-left wall.

"All of 2024 is there. Just make sure you don't mess up anything."

I pulled the previous month off the wall and brought it back out to the glass table and went through it, taking photos of invoices, then the next box, then the next box. When I got six months back I figured I'd gone far enough. If the arsonist had been angry that long, odds were they would have started burning stuff earlier.

And if I was wrong about that? Well, then I was pretty screwed. Either way, I couldn't see how I was going to start at all. So may as well narrow down how much information I was going to have to dig through.

I put the last box back in the room. It was getting late. I walked out to Amanda. "Thank you so much."

She didn't look up from her computer screen but grunted, "You're welcome." "Could I trouble you for one more favor?" I asked. "You said you have seventeen employees. Could I get a list of who they are and what their job function is?"

She turned her eyes to me as if I was the devil himself. "I need to ask my boss if that is acceptable."

"Oh, please do." I smiled. "I'm sure the police might want the information later too. In the meantime, here is my card." I pulled out my business card and threw it down in front of Amanda. "As soon as you have it ready, please email it to me."

She picked up the card, took a piece of scotch tape and taped it to the bottom corner of her screen. I was sure her boss would approve it to keep one of his biggest clients happy, and I knew Amanda, for all her huffing and suppressed rage, would get me what I needed in a timely manner.

"Thank you for your time," I said. And she nodded. "I appreciate how busy you are, so thank you for fitting me into your schedule.

"She nodded like the queen she was, deserving recognition.

Hoping I'd softened her up enough, I nodded and left. I'd swallowed the frog. Now it was time to go talk to Maria.

Saint Maria Spills the Beans

Maria greeted me with a smile like we'd known each other for years. I wondered if she and Amanda had ever met. I suspected that if they did, Maria would smile at Amanda until Amanda broke down and had to go hide in the bathroom. That was the intensity of the smile. It was peace and calm and wisdom and love. And it made me smile back.

"So sorry to keep you waiting," I said as I walked in. "I'm Sophie."

"So nice to meet you, Sophie," and the way she said it sounded so genuine I wanted to be her friend. "Can I get you anything? Water, coffee..." I looked around her little office. It was neat, and sunlit, and on her computer was a photo of two baby girls who I was guessing were her granddaughters. She was in her mid-50s, the kind of woman who had been running businesses her whole life for the substandard salary that women are paid. I really hoped that Mrs. A. was paying her what she was worth.

"No, thanks."

Maria motioned me to take a seat next to her. "Was Amanda able to help?"

"Possibly. There are just a lot of different suspects. I was hoping you might have some more concrete suspects. Death threats, anything?"

Maria shook her head. "Nothing. I mean, the man down the street got angry at her when she put the video of his dog defecating on her lawn on NextDoor, but nothing else."

"NextDoor drama. Yep, probably not the firebug, but if you could forward his name and information to me, that would be great."

"And there were some anti-Semitic things on our business Facebook page... But I just blocked them."

"What kind of things?"

"You know, this whole Israel situation... It's created some noise. Mrs. Arkbari had posted something about supporting Israel, right after the problems started, and well, after that there were some things. Like I said, I deleted them, and I also deleted her post. She really shouldn't try to do social media anyway."

"She seems like she's pretty tech-savvy. Tell me about her. How long have you been working for her?"

"I started work for her about fifteen years ago. She'd been running most of the business herself up until that point."

"Seems like a lot for one person to handle."

"She started doing it when her father was alive. Her parents sent her to school for a degree in accounting. Back then her father was buying vacant lots and building new buildings. She set up all the administration systems and collected rents. Her brother worked with her dad on the actual property construction and maintenance."

"I'm guessing her parents are long dead, so who owns the company at this point?"

"She and her brother Aaron own the business 50/50, but Aaron is in a nursing home."

"Oh, he is older than her?"

"No, younger, but he's got Alzheimer's."

My grandma got Alzheimer's. The last time I visited her in the home she didn't know who I was. I tried to tell her, and she finally decided I was my cousin Roseanne. Which was ok, because she'd always liked Roseanne more anyway. At least Roseanne had gotten married, settled down and had three children—the boy, the girl, and the spare.

I worry my mom is getting dementia. She calls me and asks me if I know what Bernice just said, repeats the whole story, then calls me back five minutes later and asks me if I know what Bernice just said. The fact that all Bernice said was that my mom didn't look a day over fifty means that Bernice is obviously a little demented herself. So I wonder on a daily basis if Alzheimer's is what's happening to my mom, and if one day it will happen to me too. Now there's a cheery thought to drag you back to the moment and actually make you listen to the person talking.

"He's in the final stages, so everything is run by Mrs. Arkbari."

I looked around the office. No one had ever thought to paint the walls anything other than pure white. The floor was painted concrete that had long since needed a repaint or actual flooring and was covered in marks from where furniture had been moved about. The desk over by the window was obviously Mrs. A's. There were no other desks, not even one for this brother who had once worked there. Apparently his desk or whatever he had used had been removed and not replaced. Due to this, I guessed I knew what the answer to my next question was.

"So, he didn't have any family?"

"No. Aaron was married young, but his wife died in an accident. She fell down the stairs when she was pregnant with their first child. So sad. He never remarried, they never had children. So it's just Mrs. Arkbari."

"Does she have children?"

"Yes, but they don't want anything to do with the business. She has three sons and she sent them all off to good schools. One is head surgeon at Cedar Sinai, one is a famous billboard lawyer, and the third's just retired after being the head of a dot com for thirty years."

"So they all think they are better than their mother?" I asked.

"Well, none of them wants for money and they all think that construction is beneath them."

"They were all very successful."

"It's easy to be successful when you have all the resources behind you." I looked at Maria a second. This was too mean, too true to be coming from her mouth. I guess she trusted me.

"How would you describe her relationship with her kids?"

"It's good."

"Really? No family disagreements of any kind?"

"None that I could mention."

So, what she's telling me is that she can't mention it, not that they don't have disagreements. I mean, hell, they are a family. Of course they have disagreements. I need to ask a better question if I want a better answer. Time to change the subject.

"So how are her grandkids doing in life?"

"The older ones are in college still. Except Melanie, of course."

People say things like this all the time, little throwaway words that mean more than the rest of the words put together. Like when my mom said Dad had been rushed to the hospital and "he was probably going to be fine." The word I took from that sentence was *probably*.

Because "probably" doesn't mean probably, and "of course" doesn't mean of course.

"Oh, what's Melanie doing?"

"Melanie married a Hassidic Jew and she's living in New Jersey in the community in Williamsburg."

"Does she still talk to her grandma?"

"Oh yes." Maria opened her phone and pulled up a picture of a young lady, maybe twenty-five, with perfect straight hair that you could hardly tell was a wig. She had a baby on her lap and two little children at her feet. Also, it looked like she was pregnant. Not sure how I felt about it, but Melanie definitely wasn't the firebug. So there was one more person I could cross off the list. Only about eight billion more I needed to eliminate.

"Do you think your boss would give me access to her social media accounts so I can go through everything?"

"I think so, but I'll double-check and let you know."

"Sounds good." I didn't feel like I'd really accomplished much. Maria was both too sweet and too forgiving to spill gossip or even think badly of others. I'd need to talk to someone else if I wanted to know the real threats to Mrs. Arkbari.

"Does Mrs. Arkbari have any household staff?"

"Yes, she has a gardener and a housekeeper that live on-site. And now that she's getting older the housekeeper doubles as her nurse and makes sure she takes her medications."

"Do you think I could speak to them?"

"I will check to see if I can set it up," said Maria. I wish I hadn't known what she was going to say before she said it. She was very predictable. She couldn't make a decision without asking the boss. She was the perfect subordinate.

"Mrs. Arkbari seems pretty spry for her age. Is she starting to slow down at all?"

"I've worked for her for a long time. So I suppose I see it better than most but she's definitely starting to slow down. Doesn't remember things like she did, that sort of thing, but she's still driving. And she gets to the office every morning."

"So she's doing great." I watched the skin tighten around Maria's eyes. Mrs. A was not doing great but she was doing ok given that she was older than dirt. I figured Maria couldn't really give me anything else until her boss approved, so I may as well ask any extra questions over the phone.

Where I Narrow the Suspects to a Few Million

I let myself out and started to go through the list while sitting in my car in the parking lot. Maria wasn't a suspect. So non-suspects were now up to eight.

Me (because I knew myself).

Harry, because, well, he's a lot of things but arsonist ain't one of them.

Circ, because he's my best friend and I've known him since I was four. Besides, he's too busy trying to save the world to worry about burning a couple of buildings.

The guy I screwed the other night (what was his name again?), because he was very, very busy at the time of the first fire. I really should remember his name. He was a good worker.

Melanie, Mrs. A's granddaughter, who was too busy being a baby incubator.

Maria, who was just too nice.

Amanda, who was not going to bother with anything beneath her, and torching a building was definitely beneath her.

Mrs. A., because I don't think she'd hire us if she'd hired someone to burn the buildings, and because she's too old to set the fires herself.

I went home to try to work. I printed all the invoices I had taken photos of at Amanda's and sorted them into piles, and laid out all the papers on my living-room floor and sat down in the middle of them trying to work out where to start.

I googled how many people were actually living in the United States. May as well eliminate people from Mongolia who lived in yurts, and bushmen in the Kalahari... in fact, anyone not actually living within two hundred miles, because how often do tourists burn down not one but two buildings while on vacation? Google told me that my suspects within two hundred miles were now down to a mere ten million or so, less the eight people I had just eliminated. So that was reassuring at least.

My head was already pounding so I decided it was time to climb into bed.

I'd had too much time lately, too much time to think. It's not good. I needed to fill the time with something. I'd already broken my vow, the one thing I swore not to do.

Pool Time Should Be Me Time

I was sitting by the pool minding my own business, working on my tan and reading through lists of contractors who had worked for Mrs. A. I had to start eliminating some somehow so I started to cross off those ones who drove more than an hour to the locations to work. This actually eliminated more contractors than I would have ever imagined. The price of housing in the city has driven most of the people who do real jobs to live further and further out and drive more and more. If you've ever hit the 5 freeway at 6 a.m. you start to appreciate how badly living here can suck.

I mean, this is LA. Everyone spends way too much time in their cars, always. And driving two hours each way from Lancaster to LA to work is one thing, driving four hours return to torch old buildings that have insurance on them? I don't think anyone is really that motivated.

So, I was looking at my laptop and trying to get a tan on the back of my legs. You would think as a not-quite-white person, getting a tan wouldn't be something I ever did. The problem is that as a not-quite-white person, if I don't get a certain amount of sun I turn yellow-gray. Yellow is a better color for a cartoon character than it is for a human being. I need a certain amount of sunlight just to look human, and I still need to take additional vitamin D to not be sick. I also need to use sunscreen on my face so I don't wrinkle like my grandma. Black don't crack. Brown does, like a photo behind glass that's been hit with a rock.

Circ came up behind me and started to hum, ever polite. He didn't want to startle me. I appreciate this. The fact that he was humming "Some Enchanted Evening" from *South Pacific* also meant that he was both embracing a stereotype and making fun of me. So pretty much a typical Circ joke. This I did not fully appreciate.

"Yeah," I groaned.

He walked to the lounger next to me and sat down. He was dressed in white. Now, it wasn't because it was after Labor Day or any of those stupid rules, but how on earth does any human being wear a white shirt? Let alone white pants? I can barely keep white socks from turning gray, and let's not talk about white pants. I am pretty sure the last time I wore white pants when I was 14, I spilled coke on them, sat in mud, then got my period. Basically, I believe white is just a challenge from the gods. I have considered that if I actually ever get married, the best color might be red. After all, it's inevitable if I am wearing white that somehow I will manage to pour red wine down my dress. Probably be while I am giving some kind of toast and then it will look like I was just stabbed and am bleeding out. Pretty much the look everyone is going for in those keepsake photos. Best to just not risk it. Not that there's any real fear of me getting hitched, let alone have a white wedding.

"So how goes the case?" said Circ.

I scowled at my computer screen. "About as well as you can imagine when everyone in the greater 9000's zip code is a suspect."

"And what about the cute guy you brought by the other night?" So Circ was going to talk about what he was really interested in.

"He didn't do it."

I rolled over and hoped I would catch some sun on my stomach. The real truth is I probably wouldn't. The sun in LA sucks. This is not something they advertise in the brochures. They don't tell the tourists about the May Gray or the June Gloom or all the other days when the marine layer covers the city. Marine layer is LA's way of saying dirty sea fog that covers the sky with a cloudless gray. And even when that burns off later in the day, or when the sun actually comes out, the sky is not clean blue but a filtered swimming pool gray with air that is rarely clean enough in the summer to allow the sun to burn the ground.

I looked at my gray, yellow skin and thought I really needed to get to Palm Springs for a weekend for some real sun. Maybe I could get away. Away from Circ, away from LA. Only problem is my mom is living out near Palm Springs and I didn't know if I was up for a visit with her.

"So," said Circ, nudging me for an answer. "Is that guy the one?"

"Nope. Not even close."

"What about your vow?"

The good thing about having a best friend is that they know all your secrets and lies. The bad thing about having a best friend is that they know all your secrets and lies. The worst thing about living with your best friend is that they can call you out on your lies.

"I blew it, ok? I knew I was blowing it. I had a hard day and..." "Oh honey, I think the vow is ridiculous."

"Ridiculous?" I sat up, pulling off my sunglasses and staring at him. "Are you saying I'm ridiculous?"

"No, honey, but your vow is. No sex unless you think the guy is marriage material? I mean, this is LA. How many guys are marriage material?""Exactly. And I'm thirty-three years old in one month and fourteen days, and I want to get married and have a family, and sleeping with losers who aren't even marriage material isn't going to get me a husband."

I was mad now and considering pushing Circ into the pool. I wondered if his white pants would become see-through.

"You know, when the right guy comes along it'll just happen."

I could feel my face snarling. "Right guy comes along? You sound like my mother. I've been waiting for the right guy since I hit puberty. And in the meantime every guy I sleep with I start having fantasies that he could be the one. That bloody oxytocin hits me and I start planning our house in the suburbs and the two and a half children we should raise. Meanwhile, all he's thinking about is whether he can get me to bend over again before his next shift delivering weed."

Circ put his hand out to touch mine. "I know you haven't had the best luck with men.""You've noticed, huh? Do you want to tell me what your tricks for picking up a boy are? I'm not rich. I'm not famous. I was born with an internal clock, and I'm rapidly approaching my expiration date. I don't need another boy to notch my bedpost. I need a man who wants to start a life with me."

"I just think you're being too hard on yourself. You aren't cut out for celibacy. No one is. Let off a little steam, don't worry about it so much, and you'll find someone.""Circ, it's not often that I hate you, but if you keep talking I will say something very unpleasant."

He sighed. "I'm only trying to help. I was hoping the last guy had actually qualified per your list." He got up to walk away. The list is something I made when I was twenty-one. I was out of the house, out of school, and looking for all the things I wanted to have to start my life. A career in the police force. A husband. A house with a mortgage I could pay off before I retired. A normal life. The list said I wanted my husband to be in the police force, have blonde hair, love animals, love kids, love his mom and dad, speak another language, like travel. Didn't seem like too long of a list. That was when I was twenty-one. Twelve years of dating later, the police force is off the list, love his mom can be a real double-edged sword, and speaking another language just gives him a way to talk behind my back and exclude me when I'm standing in front of him. Blonde hair is optional. At this point, if he has hair that's definitely a plus. Guys who shave their heads are acceptable but not preferred. Guys who shave their heads but not their chest, arms, back and sweaty man-boobs, despite the fact they look like a gorilla who was scalped, are not.

So, the list has gotten shorter and longer. Now I have added that he must be within five years of my age on the list. I've dated older men. Bernie was a great kisser, but at twenty years my senior I couldn't see myself being a widow for that long. Archie was fun, but at ten years younger he only wanted fun. He wanted to be the kid, not have the kids. So five years. Should be reasonable, but everyone who had ever hit up my online profile had always been either a decade or two older or younger.

And I'd added a couple of new line items. He must be employed, and have his own home. No more guys who are sleeping on couches and love you enough to move in with you on your second date because they are tired of using the shower at the gym. Also, I must love him and he must love me. You wouldn't think that would need to make the list but it turns out I'd loved a few guys now who just didn't love me. And there was one guy who was probably back living in the snowbelt who claimed he loved me despite my lack of interest in him.

I looked at Circ as he walked away. I wished he were straight. I loved him. He loved me. He'd make a great dad. It was such a shame all the nice men I met were out of my dating pool.

Monday's date was fundamentally a fuck boy. I found him on Tinder. And there was no way it was ever going to be anything but what it was. If I called him up, he'd definitely come over and then I'd start to imagine that there could be something more. If I called him up, we'd be in bed within the hour. And that would be both distracting and dangerous. I made the vow a long time ago. I made the vow after Paul. I'd vowed that I wasn't going to sleep with anybody unless I actually thought there was a chance for a relationship. It was just that I didn't run into anyone with whom I thought there was a chance of a relationship. So I kept breaking my vow, my own promise to myself. And ending up in one-night stands with guys who were never going to be able to commit to anything more than changing the oil of their own car.

The interesting thing is that if you can stay busy, you can ignore that you're lonely. You can forget completely that you're all alone. It's only in the quiet moments, the in-between moments when there's nothing to do and nothing dragging on your time, no one yelling they need something, that you realize that there is no other person in your life. And that you are irrevocably and completely alone. It's then that the loneliness catches you.

I was genetically predestined to be alone. As the only child of unhappy people, I would have never had anyone close if it hadn't been for Circus. He'd been born six months before me as the youngest of four boys. It was his brothers who taught him how to fight by beating him constantly, and he had taught me. When his brothers came after us we had to know how to wrestle and how to defend ourselves. I'd become skilled at the art of kicking someone in the crotch by the time

I was four because of John, Circus's oldest brother, who wouldn't let me get up off the ground.

Since he'd become rich, Circus had moved to a mansion near Pacific Palisades, thirty-five miles from the neighborhood we've both grown up in, Santa Clarita. Santa Clarita was one of those towns, a suburb city where the children are left alone by parents who commute long distances for work. It's a place where you find your tribe early or are left abandoned to fate. If you're lucky, the tribe you find helps you survive suburbia. If you're not, you and several of your friends will die. Usually overdoses in your youth on either your parents' prescription pills or some illegally obtained narcotic.

It's that kind of culture. It's that kind of California neighborhood that you see in movies. Perfect beige boxes lined up, with neatly cut grass. And swimming pools maintained in crystal clarity by Mexicans.

In order to get them to leave a hippy commune, Circ's maternal grandfather had given their family a suburban box to live in. His family did not fit in. Even more than my own. I was never comfortable in the middle-class morality. I seemed to have lacked something which would have made me enjoy the middle-class lifestyle in which I was raised. Circ's family openly defied the middle class. They didn't mow their lawn often enough. Or trim the hedges, ever. And they often had five or six cars parked directly outside on the street. Along with an old sofa or two on the lawn that hadn't quite been thrown out.

I was just lucky that he'd ended up living next to me, that the fates had intervened to give me someone to survive school with, someone who even now was trying to watch my back and look after me, and I wish I appreciated it more.

The Pool Boy is not Hot

The following morning Maria decided to take me to Mrs. A's house. Much like visiting the queen, I couldn't arrive unescorted or without an announcement.

Maria chatted the whole way. "Did you always want to be a private detective?"

Why is it that nice, well-meaning people always ask the worst questions? Of course I didn't want to be a detective. I wanted to be a peace officer in the sheriff's department and then make detective and then take some time and be a mom and a wife, and now I was nothing. None of these things. I'd burned all my bridges when I left the sheriff's office instead of going through the pain of accusing Paul of rape. After all, it would be his word against mine. And I couldn't prove anything. I'd seen the way rape cases went. There was no physical damage. I hadn't gone in for a rape kit. I'd consented simply by not hurting him, by not letting him hurt me physically, simply by lying there limp, simply by giving up on screaming no. It was close enough to consent, close enough to an alibi. So I'd left the station and the sheriff's office. "Girl couldn't deal with the stress of being a detective," they'd say afterwards.

"Life doesn't always go the way you planned," I said to Maria.

She smiled with a smile only women can share, because on some level none of us are where we dreamed we'd be. Statistically, we will never be billionaires, never marry billionaires, never run countries or Fortune 500 companies. Women who do any of these things are rare enough to be noticed. Women who rule countries are noted first as their sex and later as their function. "The woman Prime Minister of New Zealand Jacinda Ardern" would not have been famous for having a child while in office if she'd been a man. Can you image someone introducing a male head of state as "the male Prime Minister of Britain Winston Churchill"? It's just ludicrous sounding.

"I was going to college when I found out I was pregnant with my daughter, Ashley. She's in college now, studying nursing."

"What were you going to study?" I asked.

"Nursing," she said.

I asked nothing else before we arrived. The irony of women having to pass their dreams down to their children was not lost on me.

The house was not far from the office. It was a little bungalow on a large green lot with lots of parking, within an easy walk to the beach. It was white clapboard, the kind that are increasingly being torn down and replaced by glass and metal McMansions. We walked onto the property and the gardens were lovely. A flowering jacaranda and multicolored roses, and hibiscus, and curved paths made to enjoy up to a large wide porch with jasmine growing up the sides. The house was not what I expected. A ramp had been installed for Mrs. A. to come from her car but in the front were still the traditional stairs. I think I had been expecting a Beverly Hillbilly's mansion, all old and stately marble and cryptlike. "This is lovely," I said to Maria, and she nodded.

"She's lived here a long time."

We walked in without ringing a bell. Maria called out as we came in, and we walked through the living room to a kitchen where a tall, thin woman who might have been *American Gothic*'s granddaughter stood whipping eggs by hand with a whisk. "Veronica, this is Sophie. She has some questions for you."

"Yes," said Veronica in an accusatory monotone not dissimilar to her boss's. I guessed she was about forty-five, somewhere past child-bearing but not past caring. She was immaculate, with perfect nails and ironed trousers.

"Veronica is the housekeeper, and her husband Frederick does the yard work and maintains the pool," said Maria for clarification.

"We live here and look after Mrs. Arkbari," said Veronica with more than a little pride.

"Does she need a lot of help?"

"I cook, clean, do laundry. For now she is healthy but if she needs help we are here."

"How long have you worked for Mrs. A?" I asked.

She scowled at my abbreviation of her boss's name. "We have been in the employ of Mrs. Arkbari," she said, notably correcting my laziness, "for twenty-one years."

"Wow," I said. I couldn't imagine keeping a job for twenty-one years, or a relationship for that long either. She had done both—married a man, taken a job where she worked with him, and stayed married to both him and the job. I had to admire it. I also had to pretty much take both of them off the suspect list. I mean, who's going to work for a woman for twenty years and on year twenty-one go, oh well, now

I'm going to start burning down her shit because she didn't give me a big enough Christmas bonus?

"I am investigating the arsons at Mrs. A's properties. Have you seen anyone strange hanging around, or anything unusual happening in the last couple of months?"

"I see everything. Things have been normal. Mrs. Arkbari," she stared at me as she said the name, "runs a very tight ship."

"Can I speak to your husband while I am here?"

She gave me one nod and I had to wonder what she had planned for her life. As pleasant as this kitchen was, I was sure this was not it. "He is in the back."

Maria led me out the back door to a large green garden and a rectangular lap pool. Across from the pool was another white bungalow, almost identical. The man scooping the leaves off the top of the pool looked more like *Merry Old Santa Claus* than *American Gothic*. He was rotund, with a full head of white hair and a red, sunburned face. He put down the skimmer and turned to us.

"Why, hello. I am Frederick. How can I help you?"

"Hi, Frederick. This is Sophie Drake," said Maria. "She's investigating the arsons."

"Oh, those. Let's sit in the shade."

We followed him over to a lovely garden nook with some outdoor furniture shaded by a magnolia tree.

We sat down and he leaned forward. "How can I help?"

"Have you noticed anything unusual?" I asked.

"Yes. Mrs. Arkbari has been rushing out to collect the mail before I can get it and bring it in."

"I think she's talking about something like strange people hanging around," said Maria.

"No. Well, there was the man who got angry about his dog."

"What happened?" I asked.

"He kept letting his dog poop on the lawn in front, and Mrs. Arkbari noticed that there was a yellow circle starting where the grass was dying. I mean, I removed the poop but the pee-pee, well, that piece of grass was not happy."

"What happened?"

"Well, she put up a camera and put his photo on NextDoor."

"She used the internet to punish him?"

"Oh yes, she made him very mad. So he came to the house and he yelled. And she called the police."

"Did he come back?"

"No, and no more dog either."

I looked around the garden again, breathing in the fresh scent of living things. "How long have you worked here?"

"You should ask my wife. A long time. We applied for the job, and it came with the house." He pointed to the bungalow behind him. "Veronica wanted to live near the ocean, so we took the job and I work in the garden."

"Your garden is beautiful," I said.

"Thank you. It is my joy." He smiled again.

Well, I thought, *the pool boy didn't do it*. Nor did the gardener or the housekeeper, and there was no butler. So the usual cliché of guilty domestic workers in all old detective stories was just that—an old-fashioned cliché—and I was no closer to finding the arsonist.

I felt like I was digging a hole at the beach. Somewhere at the bottom was the answer but the more I dug the shallower the hole became, collapsing inwards on itself as I went. The bottom was filling with water and I was going to have to keep digging. I didn't know how far I would need to dig, or what I would find. It felt like I'd need to put myself deep into the hole and keep digging as quickly as I could, hoping that I didn't get buried down inside the hole as I went. That I didn't get so mired that I never found the truth but instead had to struggle to extricate myself and by the time I left there would be no glory. I'd just be covered in muck, with Mrs. Arkbari staring at me like I was a swamp monster and Harry wondering why he'd ever trusted or hired me.

You Need to Try Harder if You Want to Scare an Old Lady

My phone rang and I reached out to turn the ringer off or send the SCAM LIKELY caller straight to my voicemail. I mean, no one I know calls anymore. Except my mother. And I assigned her a ringtone that sounds like a fire alarm. It seemed appropriate. Friends knew to text. Even businesses were starting to text more than call. My next doctor's appointment was in two months and the dentist wanted to see me next month.

But this was someone real ringing. I didn't recognize the number so it went straight to voicemail and I started to read on the screen the message they were leaving. It's the only update that Apple has ever made that actually made my life better—being able to read the messages as they come in. It's like the old days when my mom had a message machine on the home line and we never picked up until we heard it was someone we wanted to talk to. "Hi, Sophie. It's Maria. Can you—"

Before she could say "call me back," I picked up the phone. "Hi, Maria. What's going on?"

"There's a threat in the mail."

"Ok, I will come down right now. Don't touch the letter any more than you already have."

There is something about being in a hurry in Los Angeles that makes you truly appreciate exactly how absolutely fucktastic the traffic is. I mean, people all over the world talk about traffic and complain about traffic and I have seen some godawful traffic in different cities in the world but Los Angeles has refined the traffic jam to an artform. I lived ten miles from Maria's office. The GPS told me I would get there in thirty-two minutes, so long as I avoided Pacific Coast Highway, which was currently jam-packed with tourists, all trying to get to beaches they'd seen on TV. I swear there was a time when you could get anywhere in LA in thirty minutes. That time was in the 1980s, and then again in the middle of the pandemic. So I planned to get there at some point after thirty minutes. The GPS was full of shit. It was always full of shit. Forty-five minutes later, after hitting every red light in the city and almost hitting a school bus full of kids stopping at the local school, I arrived in Maria's office.

She was sitting there, calm and smiling. I suspected even when Mrs. A. was losing her shit on her Maria was probably calm, if not smiling. But today her smile was tense at the corners and she dropped it as I walked in. "I left the letter where I opened it."

I walked over and the letter was sitting on the edge of the desk. Fully open, with the envelope thrown down next to it. In big block printing printed on someone's inkjet printer were these words: **FIRST THE BUILDINGS, THEN YOU, BITCH!**

Strangely enough, it wasn't signed. I looked at the envelope. It had a self-stick stamp. It had been postmarked in Hollywood but that didn't mean much; we knew the arsonist had been in Hollywood. After all, that's where he'd lit the fires.

"Did you call the police?" I asked Maria.

"Do you think I should? I mean, maybe I should ask Mrs. Arkbari."

"It's a clear threat," I said. "And they have more chance of finding fingerprints and matching it to the perp."

I missed not having the entire resource of the police department at my fingertips. I would have loved to put that in an evidence bag, but it was time to get the police involved. The old lady was being threatened. It would be silly not to.

"I don't think she wants the police involved."

"Call her. I'll talk to her."

Mrs. Arkbari picked up almost immediately and answered the phone with "Yes." Not "Hello," or "Good morning," but "Yes." Almost a question but not quite. More of a demand.

"Hi, Mrs. Arkbari. I have Sophie in the office. I showed her the letter I told you about. She thinks we need to call the police."

"I don't think we need to bother them. I am on my way into the office. I will be there in a minute We can talk about it then."

Mrs. Arkbari drove up in her spotlessly clean Toyota in less than a minute. We could see her driving up to the office at a speed only slightly slower than the 15-mph speed limit. She parked in front and opened the door to the car. Maria was at the door before she had it all the way open, opening it for her and subtly helping her boss out of the car and onto her walker

They walked back into the office together as if Maria walked at the same speed as Mrs. Arkbari. Maria walked her to her desk and she sat down heavily on her office chair, a shriveled-up old woman in a black gamer chair too big for her shrunken physique.

"Mrs. Arkbari," I started as she was catching her breath. "If we are going to have any chance of catching this person we need the police to run this letter through forensics looking for fingerprints. I mean, it's not like the police aren't involved already. This is an arson case. They have been notified immediately by the fire department. This is just more evidence. The faster we can find the perpetrator the less damage they can cause."

"It's just a silly letter."

"It's a threat, Mrs. Arkbari. History has taught us that we can't just ignore people who make threats. They can be unstable and danger-ous."

"It's nothing important, just words."

"Have you gotten other threats?" Suddenly I knew that she had. That she was dismissing this threat because she'd already dismissed so many others. Like my mom, who just dismissed all my dad's heart pains because he always had heart pains. So when he said his chest hurt she just told him to take some antacid. Of course, that time it wasn't heartburn, and she had called the ambulance as soon as he collapsed, but by then it was too late. I was afraid Mrs. A. had also left it too late. "How many other threats have you had, Mrs. Arkbari?"

"Not many. Just one or two."

"Do you still have them?" I asked.

"Oh no, I threw them away. Just silly things printed from a com-puter. They were always addressed to me at the office. When I am in the office I open all my own mail."

"Why weren't you in the office this morning, Mrs. Arkbari?"

"If you must know, my brother is not doing well and I went out to see him this morning. He has advanced dementia, you know."

"So sorry."

"Yes, well, he fell and broke his ankle. I went out to help quiet him while they set it."

"Sounds like a rough day," I said. "I guess you've had worse things to deal with than some anonymous threats."

"Exactly."

"So how many threats have you had exactly?"

"Four."

Maria's hand covered her mouth in shock. "How?" cried Maria. "I see all your mail."

"I open most of my mail," Mrs. Arkbari said defensively. "And since the first letter I've made sure to open the rest. They all look the same."

"So when did you start getting the threats?" I asked.

"Two weeks before the first fire."

"And you didn't think it would be good idea to mention this?"

"Why? I am sure the letters themselves didn't have fingerprints or anything."

"What did the letters say?"

"The first one called me a money-grabbing Jew and said God would punish me."

Maria gasped. "That's horrible."

"The second was worse. Similar but more hateful."

"And this is why you just destroyed the letters and didn't talk about it?" I understood now. Antisemitism was not new to her. She wasn't going to report it to the police, or show it to Maria, or even mention it. This proud old lady would take the hate and throw it away, not letting it affect her day or her life. There had been too much hate to let it change her life. Her very existence had been shaped by antisemitism.

It had sent her to a strange land as a young person, where she knew no one, to start a new life with her family. I wondered for a minute how many family members she'd lost in the holocaust. She would have lost at least some, and she would know exactly how much joy hate could take out of the world. She wasn't about to validate it by giving it space in her business, life, or home.

"I do understand, Mrs. Arkbari. I really do, but now that we have two burned buildings, and the police are already involved, we should give them this most recent letter. Maybe they can get a fingerprint off it. And even if they can't, this is evidence to help put this guy behind bars when we catch him." Mrs. Arkbari looked up at me from her chair. "You are not so bad at your job, are you, young lady?"

"Harry said I was the best of the best. Between you and me, he's wrong. I am pretty sure I am not the best, but I am pretty good."

"Pretty good may be enough," said Mrs. Arkbari. "You may call the police."

Sometimes I wish to be an Orphan

My phone rang as soon as I stepped into the car. This is not the first time this has happened. It is getting to the point where I either have to believe that my mother's become psychic after hanging out with all her tarot-reading friends or she has a spy cam pointed at me at all times.

"Hello, Mom," I said, picking up the call. After all, I couldn't let her go through to voicemail like I would my friends, or acquaintances, or just anyone. I had to pick up her call, otherwise she would just call again and again, repeatedly, until I either got a new phone number or the world ended, whichever happened first.

"Hi, darling. We are having a potluck this weekend. There's going to be a live ukulele band."

"Ukulele? Interesting."

"Yes, they are very good. There's a whole bunch of old ladies but they play great songs, like all the classics. I heard them last week."

"Ok, Mom." Since she'd moved into the retirement community, she was always inviting me to various events that I had never even considered would be entertaining. The car was finally cooling down enough with the AC that I could shut the windows. "I'm kind of busy right now. I have a case.""This is going to be the last concert, you know, and I thought you would come. I told Doreen you would be there."

"Maybe you should ask me first, Mom?"

"You always say no to everything I suggest."

"I am genuinely busy, Mom."

"You are always busy. Too busy for your mother, too busy to date, too busy to get married, too busy to have grandkids... You know, Doreen invited her grandson for this weekend. I could set you up."

"How old is Doreen's grandson?" I asked.

"Oh, he's just finished college, so twenty-three or twenty-four, I think."

"Mom, he's too young for me." I was stuck in traffic on some little surface street that used to be filled with tiny little fifties cottages and now was filled with huge multistory condo buildings. Of course, the population of the street had gone up ten times but the road was no wider or better made.

"He's not too young. You aren't that old yet. But you know, you need to hurry up. If you leave it too late you'll never have any kids and then what? You become an aged cat lady?"

"Moms, you can't say things like that. And not to me."

"You never come to visit. You know how lonely I am without your dad?"

I know she is lonely, but I am also lonely. I am also fully aware that I have no real excuse for being lonely. I have Circ, and Harry, and unfortunately my mother, who can fill every second of every spare minute if I allow them, if I allow her. It's the deep void that you think someone else can fill, that you think others might have filled in themselves, that holds the loneliness.

I suspect my mother and father were not lonely, that in their constant battles and arguments they were satisfied. That in each other they found the missing thing they were looking for. This makes me intensely sad. Not for them, because I am too selfish for that, but for me, because I don't think I can find that person, that one person who stops the ache.

I know I should feel sorry for Mom having lost her person. I want to feel sorry for her, but since she is so sorry for herself it's hard to find room to feel that for her. Also, how can I feel sorry for someone who was once whole when I don't think I will ever be whole, when I feel the broken edges of my heart tearing me up inside every day?

"I will try to come this weekend."

"The ukulele concert starts at 1 p.m. I will be sitting in the orchestra."

"You play the ukulele?"

"Yes, of course. Why else would I want you to come?" said my mother.

"You could have told me that at the beginning," I said.

"Well, I'm sure I told you. I'm in the orchestra. I only just started. John the teacher is very nice."

This is where communication between us breaks down. She tries to tell me I have to attend an event without telling me she's actually performing in the event. She went to every school play I was ever in, every parent-teacher meeting, every horrible sports day where I finished last and crying. I don't really know why she did this, but she did. She earned the credits in our relationship by being the parent in attendance. So now I have to go to the ukulele orchestra. Ukulele orchestra—sounds like an oxymoron.

"Ok, Mom. What time do you want me there?" I said knowing that she would have already planned it all out.

"Saturday at 11 a.m. we are having a potluck lunch, then the concert at 1 p.m."

Potluck lunch. Of course, food seems to get earlier and earlier in the day the older you become. I am not eager to eat my main meal for breakfast, but I'll see how it goes.

"I'll meet you at your house at ten a.m."

"Oh ok. I need to be at the clubhouse at eleven a.m. I have a dress rehearsal beforehand."

"Ok, Mom."

"And bring a side dish. Actually, bring a chicken from the supermarket. It will be better than your cooking."

"Ok," I said. Why fight, why defend myself, why explain I have actually learned to cook since that incident with the mashed potatoes when I was eleven? My mother both seems to forget that I am a fully functional adult, and that she is supposed to love me. I have to believe that she still thinks criticizing me and all my actions is a form of love. It's amazing how even after all these years small words from her can still hurt.

I got off the phone angry and distracted. It took me a minute. Mrs. Arkbari had given me permission to call the police. I was too pissed to do it myself, so I called Harry.

"Harry, Mrs. A has been holding out on us. She's been getting threats."

"Ok. What kind?"

"Letters."

"How many?"

"I saw one, at the office. I think the police should examine it. She's had others but just destroyed them."

There was a moment of silence.

"I will call it in. There's a guy I know, Detective Longe. I'll call him," said Harry. "Do you think they will find prints on it?"

"Somehow, I doubt it," I said. "If they haven't found evidence on the sites then they won't find it on a threat letter. This guy is not clumsy. He's good at details."

\"Any idea who it is?"

"No." I sighed.

"Do you need help?"

"Nope. Just following up all the leads. You deal with the police, and I'll keep going."

"Ok," said Harry and hung up. Got to love someone who doesn't drag everything out the way my mother does.

Credit Reports are a Portal to the Soul

My phone binged. Amanda had sent me a list of employees working for Bronson Construction—name, address, phone number, and social security number. I really hadn't asked for their social security numbers. I felt like she'd given them just because she wanted me to be nosy. She wanted me to pull the credit report on each and every one of them. Which, of course, I did. Starting with her.

Amanda had perfect credit. And a house that would be paid off sometime after she died. And a Macy's card. How did anyone spend four thousand dollars at Macy's? This was more confusing to me than anything. I mean, the card had no current balance but she had spent up to $4000 on it. How did one do that? Give every person on your Christmas list Chanel No. 5, then get someone in the shop to carry the bags out for you? Or was it just one dress? One of those dresses, the kind that would be on the discount rack later for $239 but when it first arrived in all its name-brand designer markup glory would look really good at a school reunion? Had $4000 been a one-dress-and-shoes? I shook my head. There was no way. Macy's just wasn't that expensive. To really waste that kind of money on one outfit she would have needed to shop in Beverly Hills. Or online at one of those silly stores that sold four-thousand-dollar shoes that were only meant to be worn once, and then only for a limited amount of time.

I did a credit check on the next one. Phil McKinley. Yes, Phil. His parents had apparently been too lazy for Phillip. He'd literally been given a name that sounded like an instruction to a gas station attendant. He also had the strangest credit report I'd seen. He had four mortgages and nothing else. There wasn't a credit card with a balance, or a car loan, or anything. I looked back to see what his job was. Project manager. Whatever that was. His name was directly under Amanda's so I guessed he was the most senior employee. After Amanda herself, of course. Or maybe it meant that he'd worked there almost as long as she had. I looked down the employee list. Seemed like everyone else had a more junior title, so maybe I should just talk to him and see if he had ideas of whom I should talk to after that.

Or maybe if I was just really lucky I'd ask him some questions, he'd admit to burning down the two buildings for some reason that I really couldn't understand yet, and then the case would be over and I could sleep in tomorrow. Well, sleep all day tomorrow and maybe the day after as well.

Ugh.

I dialed the number on the list and as I was planning to leave a message on Phil's phone, he picked up.

"Phil McKinley. How can I be of service?"

He had a manly voice with the kind of accent that reminded me of gangster movies, that rough, low, not quite West Coast accent. Exactly where he was from, I wasn't sure. Being a Californian, I'd grown up with generic Hollywood English and I wasn't good at telling where anyone born outside of the Valley was from. I wanted to ask, but asking also made me look like an idiot, and at this moment I didn't want to seem any more silly than I was already going to look after I asked all the questions I had of this man.

"Hi, Phil. I was given your number by Amanda at the office." He was quiet, listening, and said nothing so I continued. "I am investigating the arson of two of Mrs. Arkbari's buildings."

"I heard about that.""Yes. I was hoping that I could ask you some questions.""Look, I'm on-site right now. How about we meet after I leave the site tonight? Are you close to the office?""Sure," I said. Close enough. "Where and when would you like to meet?""Starbucks at Pico and Stewart?"I sighed in relief. There would actually be parking there. I thanked him silently. "Sure. What time would you be available?""I should be able to get there at 6:30," he answered.

"Ok, great. See you there.""It will be my pleasure," he said before hanging up.

Starbucks, the Best Place for First Dates

The Starbucks was one of the newer ones, built at the corner of an L-shaped strip mall in what should have been parking for the other stores. It had a drive-through. The rest of the strip mall parking lot was basically a joke. I'd been caught in traffic just trying to get into the parking lot for one of the few spots available. In terms of the Westside of Los Angeles it was fantastic, because there was free parking.

Sitting in the Starbucks, I was feeling like I was waiting for a blind date. Phil McKinley had sounded like a manly man on the phone and I was hoping he wouldn't be a pencil-necked weasel-faced little boy when he showed up. The Starbucks had the regular later-in-the-day crowd. A few single millennials who had come from work with their computers to keep working while drinking a latte and eating a sandwich that would constitute dinner, a couple of older men who simply sat there all day, perhaps writing the great American novel—perhaps—or perhaps just spent their day watching Facebook flash past the lives of others, and one awkward date in the corner. The date in question was two millennial men in business suits who kept losing track of what to say next and picking up their phones to check the time.

I have done my fair share of first dates at a Starbucks. It's safe. Neutral territory. They don't know where you live so at least they probably can't follow you home if they are in fact an ax murderer. And you know what you are going to order in advance, so you don't get served something you want to spit out mid-bite.

This is a definite advantage.

There was that time I went on a first date in a bar. I discovered a few things.

1. That the young man I'd been online chatting with was at least three inches shorter than he said he was on his profile, which meant that even though I am five foot two, in my 4-inch platform boots I was taller than him. As a short woman, I am unaccustomed to grown men being so short that when they hug me they get squashed into my boobs, and,

2. Men who insist on having a first date at a bar may be alcoholics.

3. Also, get to the venue early and if he's already there drinking just get back in your car and drive off, and,

4. Most importantly, the life lesson that jalapeno margaritas suck. They also burn horribly when you find yourself gagging and the evil that is lime, peppers, chili and tequila shoots back out through both your nose and mouth.

At thirty-two, I have had more first dates than my mother had dates in her entire life. After all, she met my dad when she was twenty-two, they got married when she was twenty-four, and they lived happily ever after. Or at least till he died. At least that's how she wants to tell the story. If happily ever after includes regular dish-throwing and screaming matches over inconsequential amounts of money, then they were very happy.

My phone beeped. It was Phil. "I'm here. I'm wearing a red shirt. I'll go to the bar and order a drink. Do you want anything?"

Sensible man. I responded that I didn't need anything. He was not disappointing when he walked in. His voice and body matched, both large and strong. He ordered a latte and turned. I waved and he walked over. I stood. He was a solid-looking man, normal on the attractive side, with a masculine jaw and pretty blue eyes.

"I'm Sophie. Thanks for coming."

He nodded and shook my hand. His hands were hard and calloused in a way that is no longer normal in our world. Or at least not normal in Los Angeles, California, where half the guys I see have nice manicures and far better cuticles than the ones I rip off bleeding with my teeth.

"Nice to meet you," he said, sitting down. "So how can I help you?"

"I am investigating the arson at Mrs. Arkbari's buildings and I am trying to find out a little about how the maintenance work is done on her properties."

"Ok," he said, putting his hands up on the table. I found myself looking down at his hands. Capable hands, I thought. It had been a nice handshake, perfect in fact—warm, dry, not too long, not too hard, not too limp. Oh, damn, my hormones were definitely running overtime. I could only think about exactly how capable his hands might be.

"What can I tell you? We have a small crew and we do most of the little repair stuff ourselves. Our guys are all kind of maintenance men, general duty, a little plumbing, a little drywall."

"But there were bills for a plumber and an electrician at the two properties."

"We try to keep the costs down by not getting out the specialists unless we need to, but most of Mrs. Arkbari's places are pretty old. The two that burned were at least 50 years old and they start having bigger problems."

"DRINK FOR PHIL!" yelled a voice from the bar.

"I'll go get my drink. Be right back."

I pulled out my folder and pen while he grabbed his drink. I needed something to look at that wasn't his hands, or his pretty eyes. They were deep blue with long, dark lashes, and I've always been a sucker for dark blue eyes. He was a suspect, for God's sake, and as I watched him walk to the bar I found myself wondering if he was a boxer or brief guy.

He came back quickly and I looked down so as not to ogle him in a way he could notice. "Has your entire crew worked at Mrs. Arkbari's properties that burned down?" I asked, pushing the list of men in front of him from my folder as if he didn't know the names of his own crew.

He looked down at it. "In the last six months or so I'd say most of the crew could have possibly been on-site, except Marco, Jimmy and Fauli. They work the properties in Santa Monica only. And not Manuel because he's only been on the crew a few weeks. The guys who usually work Hollywood are Rob, Freddie, Armando, Steve, Mario and Peet. But I can go through the logs and confirm who has been on-site recently."

Four people I could cross off my list. Should have made the list feel shorter, but it didn't.

"Have you been to these sites?" I asked, hoping he'd say no.

"Oh yes. I am the one who has to verify if we need to call out a specialist. I did the inspections and called the electrician and the plumber that you saw the bills for. And we also redid some apartments there and I supervised that."

Well, damn, definitely a suspect. Suppose I'd better start that list, since the probably-not-a-suspect list was running out of applicants.

"Do you know anyone who might have beef with Mrs. Arkbari?"

"We just fix the properties. I guess she talks to Amanda but I've never spoken to her directly. She's not my boss, just a client."

"Do you know if any of your guys have met her?"

"I wouldn't think so. Not sure." He brought his coffee to his mouth and took a long drink. "I doubt it."

Seemed to me like whoever had burned down Mrs. A's buildings probably had beef with her. And it was really hard to hate someone if you'd never met them. I mean, even my mother was loveable and friendly if you didn't know her well.

"So no one would have had any personal grudge against her?" Ok, it was a dumb question and I knew it even as I was saying it, but I was getting distracted again. He was actually a very attractive man, and not at all pretty (except for his eyes). It had been a while since I'd met a guy who obviously didn't have head shots of himself in his glovebox. It was just kind of sexy.

"Not that I know. But if you want to talk to the guys, you can."

"Great." I should absolutely do that, even if it was going to take forever. "Yes, I probably should."

"We meet at the office on Monday at seven if you'd like to come."

"Seven a.m.?" I could feel my soul sinking downwards into a swirling nightmare of alarms ringing and ringing. "Sure, I'll be there, if you don't mind."

He looked me straight in the eye and said, "I am looking forward to seeing you again."

I smiled that smile you make when you don't want to start doing the girly giggly thing but you have small butterflies in your tummy. He really did have nice eyes. "I will be there. Before I go, is there anything you can tell me about the plumbing or electrical companies?"

"They are pretty good people. We've worked with them for years. I don't know which guys came to the job site and did the work on Mrs. Arkbari's place but I can find out for you if you'd like."

"That would be amazing." Someone was actually offering to help. Ok, maybe he was actually my prime suspect and he was just trying to divert my attention from his own crimes, but at this point I would have accepted help from Charles Manson. Millennial date men had stood up and were shaking hands. That was over. No one was getting any nookie tonight over there. And I wasn't getting any either. But it didn't mean I wasn't going to go home thinking about it. Phil and I walked out to his car, which was, of course, a pickup truck. I hopped back in my car, turned the radio up as loud as I could and drove back to the office with Joan Jett and the Blackhearts telling me what I should have done.

Morning Meetings Melt My Brain

The morning meeting at Bronson Construction started at seven a.m. I arrived at eight. Amanda was ready for me when I arrived for the meeting. Despite the owner of the company being there, this was her meeting. She was in charge. She held the door open for me and I walked in. Phil was there, and the whole crew. All seventeen of them. The only ones I was really interested in were the ones who worked the Hollywood area. So Rob, Freddie, Armando, Steve, Mario and Peet, and I had no idea which of these men they were.

The owner of the company, Francisco, stood at a whiteboard in front of the room. Everyone sat around on the chairs that were available, and leaned on desks and against the walls. It was way too many people for such a small room and I realized that there really was no space at all for me. Suddenly I saw Phil inch the guy next to him over and motion for me to join him.

I found myself against the wall next to him, too close. I could smell him and tried not to move, not to get any closer. He smelt like wood and soap and man. It was an interesting smell, different from the Axe body spray the last Gen Z fuck boy had bathed in. I could feel Phil standing next to me, the heat coming off him. He made me feel so very, very small.

"Thanks for coming, everyone," said Francisco. "Mrs. Arkbari, our biggest client, is having issues with her buildings. She's hired a private detective to investigate why two of her buildings have been torched. Sophie Drake," he pointed at me, "will be talking to everyone today, or giving you a call. So I want you to cooperate."

Amanda stood up and picked up a list. "Rob, Freddie, Armando, Steve, Mario and Peet, could you all stay here to talk to Sophie. Everyone else is free to go, but I will be giving Sophie your numbers and she may be calling you if she has any questions. Please pick up her calls, and let me know if you need any help reaching anyone, Sophie." She said my name like we were friends, like I was someone she knew. Like we actually liked each other. It seemed a little strange and somewhat off-putting coming from her mouth. But somehow it wasn't forced and the other people seemed to believe her.

"Is there anything you'd like to say to the group?" Francisco asked.

I peeled myself off the wall, rubbing against Phil as I walked out into the center of the room. "Hi. If anyone has any information at all about any of Mrs. Arkbari's properties, if you've seen anyone checking them out or looking them over, please give me that information. Anything I can find out may solve this investigation. And I want to thank you in advance for your help." Amanda got up and started directing people. "Ok, everyone whose name I did not call out, you are free to go. Your work roster is updated in BuildOps. As always, any questions, please let me know."

The guys started to file out past Amanda's desk quietly like the teacher had just dismissed them from class and they would get a detention if they spoke before they hit the playground.

Amanda walked over to me and took my arm. "You sit here," she said, pointing to the glass conference table in the center of the room. Francisco sat down at his desk, facing the glass conference table. The men I was due to talk to stood around, and it looked like the most awkward setup ever to conduct an investigation, let alone an interrogation. One of these men was my most likely suspect, and there was no way I was going to find out who. Not by talking to them in the middle of an office while their boss and his assistant stared at the back of their head and their co-workers listened in, making sure all their stories jived.

"Oh, thanks so much, Amanda, but I need just a bit of privacy. You," I said, pointing to one of the men standing there. "What's your name?"

"Armando."

"Great. Come with me. Let's go take a walk." I walked out of the office with the wrath of Amanda burning a hole in the back of my shirt. I stopped at my car, grabbed out a clipboard, walked out towards the park across the road and sat down on a park bench.

Armando joined me, sitting across from me. "So what do you want to know, lady?"

"What do you do?" "Mostly I do drywall. You know, patch and fix and paint stuff." He was at this moment looking down and digging paint out from under his fingernails.

"Have you ever met Mrs. Arkbari?" I asked.

"Who's that?"

"The woman who owns the properties that burned."

"Oh yeah, her. No," he answered, and I was sure even if he had he wouldn't remember or care. He also looked like he didn't care if I kept talking to him all day or just left him alone. Armando looked like he'd reached that point in life that only the wealthy thought was success. He'd reached the point where he was Zen. Not because he had given away every care with lots of meditation and vegan cuisine but because life had been so hard that he'd stopped rolling with the punches and just let them roll over him. I looked at his hard, scarred hands. This wasn't a man who would burn a building. This was a man who would put out a fire.

"Do you have any kids, Armando?"

"Three boys, two girls, and two grandbabies." He looked up at me for the first time. "They is good kids but they all live in my house. The babies no sleep."

I scratched Armando off my list. Any man who was supporting that many people and living with crying babies did not have enough energy to torch a property.

"Thanks for talking to me, Armando. Can you send the next guy out to talk to me?"

"Ok, miss." He stood up and walked back to the office in a loose-legged gait, and a young man who looked like he could bench-press me started to walk over.

"Hi. Take a seat," I said, pointing to the huge black man who now sat across from me. "What's your name?"

"Frederick Johnston the Third, ma'am, but everyone round here just calls me Freddie."

Now, I don't in general like being called ma'am but when it's done in a low southern accent by a true southern gentleman who's been well raised by his mama to call every man sir and every woman ma'am, I find myself just a little warmed by the sweet molasses drawl.

"Hi, Freddie," I said, checking him off on my notes. "What is it you do?"

"General construction. You know, everything from putting in a door to installing cabinets to framing up a wall to putting on the drywall."

"Drywall, like Armando?"

"I don't do the finish stuff, usually, like Armando. That man's a genius with a putty knife. But we do work together. Usually I'll put up the drywall, and tape it, then he'll finish it while I keep going."

"Do you remember the last time you were working at either of the two properties in Hollywood?"

"You mean the ones that burned, ma'am?"

"Yes." I was beginning to wonder if he was stalling for time by asking that. Of course the ones that burned. Maybe the sweet southern drawl was just the way he made sure he was never suspected. I mean, I was sure that all over the South, well-spoken men with beautiful accents were in jail for beating their wives to death or shooting a convenience store clerk. Having a nice voice didn't make you innocent. Televange- lists were proof of that. Some of them were some sweet-talking dudes.

"I was in the apartment building about two weeks ago. We was all over there. The tenant in the upper apartment had been evicted, and then when the police took them out there was holes in the walls, and they'd burned up the wall behind the stove. The plumbing was bro- ken. It was a mess, ma'am." An angry evicted tenant. Damn, I hadn't even heard about that. There were some more names for the list. I'd need to talk to Maria to find out who'd been evicted in the last few months. If I lost my rent-controlled apartment in LA, I'd be ready to burn down the building and the woman who owned the place.

"Who was working with you to fix it up?"

"Oh, it was pretty much the whole crew. And we had the plumber and the electrician too. They'd installed their own AC, then took it outta the wall and taken it with them, so the AC guy too came and put one in, you know, proper. Took us a solid week to get the place ready to rent, ma'am. While we was fixing it up the owner had us pull out the whole kitchen and replace everything. Don't think anyone had done anything to the place since it was built. It was a whole bunch of work, ma'am."

"Have you ever met the client, Mrs. Arkbari?"

"I think so. I believe she was in the office once talking to Amanda when I was there. Sure enough she didn't talk to me, though."

"Ok, thanks, Freddie. Can you send the next guy out?"

"Surely, ma'am," he said, getting to his feet in a slow, deliberate way. I wasn't going to rule Freddie out. Here was a man who had met Mrs. A, and by the quiet in his voice I suspected she had treated him like he was furniture. He was a proud man, and I couldn't tell how that would affect him but I suspected that all his ma'ams and sirs hid his rage.

Mario was the next guy walking towards me. He came at me chest puffed out, annoyed. The tight shirt, gold chain, and tattoos on his arms reminded me of a little boy's idea of what a man should look like.

"So what you want ta know?"

"Just wondering what you do."

"Bit of this and that. Tiling, painting, helping hang drywall, you know, bit of everything."

"Ever met the owner of the properties?"

"Nope. Don't usually meet anybody 'cept the people who live there."

"Did you meet the people who lived at the apartment on Virgil?"

"Oh, they hate us. We showed up to work out what to repair that first day and they was still there pulling their stuff out and they were screaming at us telling us to go fuck ourselves."

"Does that happen often?"

"Sometimes. People don't like getting kicked out of their homes. They think the rich people who own the place don't really need the rent, ya know."

"Yeah, maybe they don't. Can I give you a call if I have any more questions?"

"Can't really stop you, can I? But yeah, I'd take a call. Why not?"

"Thanks, Mario. Send out the next guy, will you?"

I was starting to feel like an HR person interviewing people for the position of arsonist. Much like an HR person, I couldn't really ask the questions I wanted to ask. In the same way that the director of personnel couldn't ask if they would work hard and be good employees after they started work at the company, I couldn't ask them how many buildings they'd torched and whether or not they hated rich old ladies. I wiggled around on the park bench I'd sat myself down on. My butt was starting to hurt, the August sun which had been hiding behind the gray morning gloom was now awake and trying to burn a hole in my scalp, and what was more annoying was that I didn't feel like I was getting anywhere with this.

Rob came out next. He looked like all the kids I went to school with—tall, thin, confused, and a little stoned at 8.30 a.m. He was just cool enough to sit himself sideways on the end of the park bench so I had to turn and squint into the sun to talk to him. I decided instantly that I hated him, which meant he was probably, but not definitely, innocent.

"I'm Rob," he said, tossing his hair back a little as if I should perhaps recognize him. "How can I help you?"

"Um..." He'd put me off my game, talking first. I hate it when that happens. I want to be in control of every situation and now I had to hold myself back so I didn't get aggressive and angry. "What do you do, Rob?"

"Oh, I'm like a fix-it guy, you know. There ain't nothing I can't do, you know."

"What did you work on at the Virgil apartment building?"

"Oh, I don't think I worked there."

"How about the laundromat on Vermont?"

"Nope, I don't think I worked there either, you know."

"So, if you were there, what would you have been doing?"

"Maybe some carpet laying or tile work, or helping install light fixtures. Usual stuff, you know."

"How do you feel about rich people?"

"Oh, I think they are pretty cool. I mean, I'm planning to be one of them one day so I better think that way, you know. Positive mindset. I keep a picture of Elon Musk on my wall, man. And all my extra money goes into crypto. Do you have any Euretheum? It's going to totally blow up, you know."

Looking at Elon Musk every day sounded like some kind of torture, but who was I to say? I would ask Circ about the Euretheum. "Did you ever meet Mrs. Arkbari?"

"Who's that?"

"Woman who owns the buildings."

"Oh yeah. No, but sure, she's cool, you know." I nodded. One more "you know" or "man" and I was probably going to smack him. "Great, Rob. Thanks for talking to me. Could you send the next guy to see me?"

"Sure thing." Rob wandered back to the office, pulling a vape out of his pocket and taking a couple of quick hits before he walked back inside. There were only two left. Peet and Steve.

When the short Asian man came out of the office I couldn't begin to guess which he would be. Turns out he was Steve.

"Yes, I do all the carpentry. You know, cabinets and stuff."

"Did you work on the two properties that burned?"

"Just the apartment building. When we did the entire remodel everyone worked there. I did the kitchen cabinetry and bathroom cabinets."

"So Rob was at the project?"

"Oh yes, he was helping haul the cabinets up and down the stairs for me. We wanted to turn the apartment around really fast so we were all on-site for about a week."

Ok, so Rob had lied to me about that. What else had he lied about? "Did you meet the tenants that were being evicted?"

"Yes. They refused to leave, kept sitting on the steps. I had to step over them. We had to call the police to take them away"

"Did you ever meet the owner of the properties?"

"The old lady? Sure. She came to look at our work when we were working on the apartment remodel. Checking up on us, I guess. I also saw her back on a different building we were remodeling for her. She came in, grunted, and left. Usually she comes with a sweet-faced Mexican lady."

"You're sure she came to the job site?"

"Yes, of course. We had just about finished when she came. We were all there on-site. Rob was cleaning up boxes, Armando was painting the last couple walls, Mario was sealing the grout. I remember because we had until five p.m. to finish it and she showed up at three and said we should be done already."

"Wow, that must be annoying."

"I don't really care but I know Phil told her off, told her that we'd been given the rest of the day to finish and she had no right inspecting the property until the next morning, and that if she wasn't careful we'd get some paint on her Gucci shoes."

Phil never told me that Mrs. Arkbari came to the jobsite. I looked down for a moment to my notebook. He'd said he'd never talked to her directly. Phil was lying.

"Interesting. How long have you worked on her properties, Steve?"

"Well, I've been with the company for eight years, so eight years, I guess. I know she owns a whole bunch, but I'm not really sure which ones they are exactly. I didn't even know she owned the laundromat and the apartment building on Virgil till they both burned."

"Thanks, Steve. Can you send Peet?" I said, standing. My ass was really hating the concrete picnic table. So I walked around slowly, trying to get the feeling back into both of my ass checks before I sat down again. Peet was a little man in his forties who positively hopped towards me. It seemed like one of his legs was just a bit shorter than the other and rather than let it slow him down he just threw himself forwards and hopped to keep up with his leading leg.

He walked over and offered me one of his dry, scarred hands to shake. "It's a pleasure to meet you, Miss Sophie. I was beginning to think you'd forgotten about me. How do you do?"

"I do ok, Peet. How about you?"

"Oh, God is good. I keep busy and healthy, so everything is great. The other guys said you wanted to know what each of us do. Well, I do a bit of everything, you know, but mostly I help out where I'm needed. And that apartment, well, it was disaster, let me tell you. I had to demo the interior walls, the kitchen, and the bathroom, and take all that stuff out. Such a pity, because all my work just went up in smoke, you know. I mean, we made that apartment look great. It had nice, clean, white subway tile and vinyl flooring, and the walls were a soft gray. We even changed out the windows for those new energy-efficient ones and put in a new mini-split AC. It was a nice place, it was. Such a pity. Such a pity."

Peet was starting to remind me of the human version of Tigger from *Winnie the Pooh*. I suspected that he wasn't even faking it, that this was who he was most days of the week most weeks of the year.

"So, Peet, do you remember Mrs. Arkbari coming to inspect the property on the last day?"

"Oh yes. Not a happy woman, I think. I mean, I've seen her at other job sites too. Usually comes with Maria. Maria's such a lovely woman. They come to see if we have done a good job. And you know we have because we keep getting more work from them. I mean, I didn't know the lavanderia across the street was hers too. I've done so much work in there, you know, when they had that flood and we had to go in and strip out the flooring and put in the new drains through the floor, and then the tiles and the drywall."

"When was that?"

"Not sure... Maybe last year. It was a big job. We were all working there for that one too."

"All of you? Are you sure?"

"Well, Armando wasn't there—that was the week he had COVID—but the rest of us were there for sure. I heard she doesn't rent that laundry, that it's one of the old lady's side hustles. I would like to have a laundromat as a side hustle. It would be nice to just take the money out of the machines. I would be able to spend more time at church and on my hobbies."

I wondered for a moment how Peet could know this. Who had told him that the laundromat business belonged to Mrs. A? Had someone mentioned it in passing?"Oh yes, wouldn't it be nice? What are your hobbies, Peet?"

"Well, I rebuild cars. I have a classic Chevy Bel Air hot rod and I am working on a Chevy Impala. It's a rat rod for now but I want to deck it out all the way when I have the money."

"Did you also see the tenants who had to be evicted?"

"No, I don't think so... Not sure... There were tenants that had to be taken by police at a different property, an apartment block on Fountain."

"What do you think of Mrs. Arkbari having all that money and evicting people?"

"It's unfortunate but it's not my place to say what is in the minds of others. Only God knows our true nature and he is the only one who can judge us. It is not my place to judge but only to be judged for my own actions. And in this as in all things I am responsible and must engage with the world in the way I see best so that in the end I am a force for Good and for God and when my day comes I will be judged as a righteous man."I almost wanted to yell Amen. This guy was a hell of a preacher for all his hopping, walking and smiling face. He was fun. And also he'd contradicted pretty much everyone else's story. I knew less for sure now than I had before I started questioning everyone. All I knew for sure at this point was that I was starving, that I needed much, much, more coffee, and that I'd have to talk more to Amanda.

Breakfast and a Hole in One

I walked back into the office with Peet and he grabbed his keys and left in the work truck.

"I have some time. Do you have any more questions for me now that you've met everyone?" asked Phil.

"I do but I am also deeply in need of food and coffee. Do you want to come to Starbucks with me?"

"Hop in my truck. I know somewhere closer and better."

I breathed a sigh of relief at putting Amanda off for later and hopped up in Phil's truck. It was clean but not too clean. There was an empty Starbucks cup in the cup holder, and a clipboard fallen down in the passenger's side floor. I picked it up. Phil had written all over it in a beautiful delicate script, the kind my mother always wanted me to have. The kind that no one has. I was sure they were his notes. I'd feel pretty stupid if this was his girlfriend's writing.

He turned on the motor and was pulling out of the parking lot. "You have nice handwriting," I chanced."Yeah," he said, almost embarrassed. "My mom was a school teacher and she made me practice and practice my cursive." He swung right and we were heading towards the ocean. "So if this whole being a building contractor fails I can always get a job doing calligraphy. I hear illuminated manuscripts are a growing field."

I giggled.

He made a quick left and right. He drove confidently but smoothly. I found myself relaxing. His radio was on a playlist from before my youth but recognizable. He pulled the car into a parking lot and I was surprised to find that instead of taking me to a diner or a bougie breakfast coffee place he'd brought me to a golf course.

I jumped out of the car and followed him through the gates and hard left into the Penmar restaurant. We seated ourselves and a young Latino man brought us menus. "The food is great here," said Phil.

"Do you do lattes?" I asked the waiter.

"Of course," he replied.

"Ok. I'll start with a double.""Oat milk, almond milk..."

Before the waiter could list off the rest of my options I said, "Real milk."

"Make it two," said Phil.

We sat on an outside table in the sun and I focused on studying the menu.

While I was waiting for the drink to come I figured I'd ask Phil some of the questions that were bothering me now that I'd talked to his guys.

"So the guys tell me that the last time they fixed up an apartment at Mrs. Arkbari's place on Virgil the tenants had just been evicted by the police and were still around."

"Yeah. Mrs. Arkbari is always in such a hurry to rent her places again. She gives us very short timelines and sometimes we run into the people that have been evicted. I mean, if she'd just wait a day or two... but she doesn't."

"So did these people threaten your guys?"

"I wasn't on-site till later. Peet said the young woman was just sitting on the stairs crying, holding a baby. He had to step over her to get to the apartment. The older lady, grandma I suppose, screamed at him. And the two guys just tried to block their way. They were the ones the police took away so we could get in."

"Sounds dramatic."

"It happens. Anyway, we only had a week to remodel the whole apartment, so we had to move."

The waiter came with the lattes and water. It was in a big, wide cappuccino cup and I took a swig, leaving myself with a milk mustache. Phil smiled and pointed and I wiped it off, reminding myself to sip, not gulp the drink. "So what kind of shape was the apartment in? The boys say it was rough."

"About normal for a rent-control place. Pretty much everything built before 1978 is subject to rent control. Rent can only go up like 4% a year. Well, more now, but still... cheap. So landlords don't really make repairs on rent-control places, not unless they are necessary. These people had been there a long time. So it had been painted maybe twenty years ago."

"But you did more than paint?"

"Yeah, well, if we do enough repairs it changes how much the place can be rented out for when it goes back on the market. So we did a full rehab. That way she could rent it for way more."

"So what happened to the people who got evicted?"

"I don't know. Don't want to think about it."

The waiter was back staring at us with that face that said order now. "Are you ready to order?" He looked so anxious about it I kind of wanted to say, "No, give us another five minutes," but I was genuinely hungry.

"I'll take the huevos rancheros, eggs cooked hard as possible, and another latte."

"I'll do the classic egg breakfast, eggs over easy, with potatoes and pancakes."

"Great," said the waiter, grabbing the menus off us. I miss the days when waiters used to write things down. They all seem to think memorizing orders is some kind of Olympic event that they are all in training for. All I know for sure is that thirty percent of the time I get something different than what I ordered.

"Does Mrs. Arkbari ever come to the properties you are working on?"

"She's been to a few."

"I hear that she owns the laundromat. That it's her business, not something she rents out."

"That's interesting," said Phil, as if this was genuinely news to him.

"So did she come to that one?"

"I don't think so. We didn't do much there—just some plumbing issues; had to change out some pipes. I think her assistant came to that one. Maria. Nice woman."

"Did she come to the apartment?"

"Maybe. I don't think so." Everyone was telling me a different story but I'd spent long enough in the police to know that was normal. Two people seeing the same incident wouldn't remember it the same way. Even though it made me suspect everyone, it didn't really mean that anyone was deliberately lying. It just meant that I had no idea what had really happened. If two of the guys had told me the same story exactly I would have had to worry that they had compared notes. The only way that we end up with corroborating witnesses on the stand in court is because their stories are similar enough and the lawyer works with them to make sure they say the right thing. The right thing is more important for a jury than it is for me.

Mrs. A. did sometimes go to job sites. Most everyone had met her, except Mario, who claimed to have never met her. Maria also went to job sites, sometimes possibly with Mrs. Arkbari. The tenants who left this apartment were pissed. But how much work would some evicted tenants need to do to find out not only who owned their apartment building but also find out what other buildings she owned and torch them?

Not that I could rule them out. I'd ask Maria for the list of all the evicted tenants but it was still more likely that it was someone who had worked on the properties. Someone who'd met Mrs. A. I mean, meeting her hadn't made me love her, and I like to think of myself as a person who tries to get along with everyone. After all, I still take my mother's calls, so I obviously have a deep well of empathy that I hide from the world.

The food arrived and we both dug in unapologetically. I looked over at this man I was eating breakfast with. He could be the person who'd torched the buildings. I really hoped he wasn't. "What can you tell me about Mario?"

"He's a decent worker, shows up on time, does what he's asked to do."

"Do you trust him?"

"With what? That's relative. I think I'd let him drive my car but not date my daughter."

"You have a daughter?"

"Nope, no kids. Single. Just a figure of speech." He smiled at me, and he had a nice smile, a warm smile.

"You know it's probably one of your guys that is torching the buildings," I said bluntly.

"Yep, I understand the math, but I can't imagine any of them doing it. Why would they?"

"That's what I want to ask you. Someone has been sending her threats. This is personal for someone. Any idea who?"

"Wow. No. I mean, I'll think about it. But that kind of makes me think that it can't be anyone in my crew. I mean, that kind of hate... not sure if any of them could hide that. They don't know this lady well enough to be that pissed. It's not like she's their direct boss, or former girlfriend."

He wasn't wrong. I needed to work out what motive anyone had for burning these buildings. It was becoming obvious that they hated her, that it was, as I had suspected all along, personal. But who had a motive? They worked occasionally on her buildings and she occasionally showed up while they were working, but that was hardly a motive. I really needed to talk to Maria about the evicted tenants. They had much more reason to be angry than the guys working on the building.

"How about Armando?" I said, looking down at my notes and wanting to cross someone off. "Did he have COVID during the repair of the laundromat?"

"I'd have to check. Not sure. We've had a lot of guys out since the pandemic. Used to be they'd all come to work sick or healthy, but not anymore. If they come to work sick everyone else yells at them. It's hard to keep a crew at work or even keep to a deadline when half your guys can get sidelined because there's an outbreak of the flu at their kid's elementary school."

"Would any of your guys know how to burn a building?""Sure, I think so. They know how to build one, basically. They know the structure, most of them. Maybe all of them. So yeah, burn the bit that holds it up. Not so complicated.""Does anyone fly small planes?""I'm working on my pilot license. I am pretty sure I'm the only one."I looked up from my eggs at the man I'd been contemplating taking home and having for dessert. That was not good. Not good at all.

"Does your boss fly too?""Oh hell, no. He thinks I'm crazy. He saw a student pilot kill himself and his instructor a few years back and he's convinced I'm going to kill myself. No one even wants to come up with me. Do you fly?""Only when I have to and in as big of a plane as possible, thanks," I said, wondering if he knew he had just gone to the top of the suspects' list. "What can you tell me about the electrician contractor and plumbing contractor?"He pulled out his phone and read off, "I looked into it. Mike's Way Plumbing and Speedy Spark Electrical worked on both properties. They are the only ones that did.""Well, what can you tell me about them?"

"Oh, Mike's a great guy. He runs a pretty small shop—just him, his son, and one assistant. He's caught the flying bug too, so we go up together sometimes to get enough flight hours." Ok, so Mike gets added back into the list. At least Phil wasn't my only suspect. I looked at him over my food. Did I find him more attractive now that I thought he might actually be a criminal?

I need to ask myself these questions. Because there is nothing like the bad-boy complex every woman has been fed since *Rebel Without a Cause.*

"Ok, I will need to talk to Mike and maybe his crew. What about Speedy Spark?"

"The owner there is Joe. He has a lot of trucks and crews. So I don't know exactly who came out. But if you talk to Tina—she's in the office and she can help you out. I already sent her a message to say you'd be calling."

"Wow, that's awesome, thanks."

"I'll AirDrop you the contact cards for both."

"Thanks," I said, looking down and accepting the information to my phone. I looked out of the restaurant to where old men were putting balls into small holes. It almost looked like fun, walking around on the putting green in the shade of huge pine trees. Honestly, I wished I was out there with them, with a clear direction where to aim and some idea of where the end goal was. If I knew where I was heading I might even be able to hit a hole in one. At the rate I was going, I was going to be running around after my tail forever and never figure out who had torched the buildings. I was really hoping it wasn't Phil. If it was him he was being very helpful to line up other suspects for me.

"You don't happen to be free this Saturday night, would you?" He looked over at me, making sure to make eye contact with his large, disturbingly pretty eyes.

"So sorry," I said reflectively, because I couldn't date a suspect. Then remembered I actually did have a prior commitment. "I am going to be visiting my mom on Saturday. It will take all my strength."

He smiled. "Well, whenever you are free, the invitation stands. I'd like to take you to dinner." I smiled back. "That would be lovely." *As soon as I have cleared your name and know for sure you aren't wanted by the authorities for trespassing and felony arson.* "I'll let you know."

Back to the Witches' Lair

Phil dropped me back at the office to talk to Amanda and pick up my car after a ride that had been much more intimate than the ride out to the restaurant.

Obviously Phil was the arsonist. He had to be. He flew small planes, so he had access to the accelerant. And also because I thought he was attractive and nice, and my radar on that kind of thing couldn't be trusted at all.

I hadn't been able to trust my radar since Paul. Before him I had always believed I knew good people. Before Paul I had always believed that I was a good judge of human beings and that my gut knew the answers.

I remembered when Paul had first come to the station. It was before I was made detective. I'd been living in the mountains above Los Angeles for about six months. He was sweet and sexy. He asked for me to work on his cases. And then, when I made detective, he'd asked if I could be his partner. I was so excited. I'd made detective. I was living in a beautiful place. And Paul wanted me. Wanted me as his partner. And he wanted me in other ways too. My life was everything I could want.

When Paul asked me out he said we needed to keep it a secret because we didn't want to have any talk in the station, or deal with any fraternization rules. When we met for drinks at his house and he held me down and raped me he said I needed to keep it a secret because who would believe me?

It was obvious I couldn't trust my instincts. My instincts said Phil was innocent and somewhat nibbleable. So the arsonist was obviously Phil. He seemed sweet and sexy, and into me. So obviously a criminal. Now all I had to do was prove it.

What was his motive? What was anybody's motive? The only people who had a really good motive were the people who were evicted, and I would still need to follow up on that. I texted Maria to ask if I could come visit her later in the day.

I took a deep breath and walked into Amanda's office.

She ignored me and I stood in front of her desk waiting for her to respond. The sweet smiling woman she'd been for all the men earlier was gone. She was back to being queen bee and bitch over all she surveyed.

I coughed and she tipped her head to look down her nose at me. "You came back." As if I was some wicked woman who had gone off with Phil for a little afternoon delight. I wondered if she was jealous and would like to have gone off with him, or anyone, for a little afternoon delight, or just gotten out of the office for coffee. The more she hated me the sorrier I felt for her. It was a strange sensation.

"Yes." I looked over at her boss still sitting at the desk in the corner of the room. "Phil said you could give me the contact information for all the people I spoke with today, as well as the information for Mike's

Way Plumbing and Speedy Spark Electrical. And the timesheets broken out for all the men I spoke with today for the last six months." Ok, Phil had already given me Mike's Way and Speedy Spark, but that just meant he was being suspiciously helpful. And I needed to give her something to do. Wouldn't pay for her to think that someone had done an end run about her when she was obviously so busy trying to be the company's defensive back. In fact, the whole defensive line, and she was doing a pretty good job at just being defensive.

She turned to her boss, as I knew she would, looking for someone else to say no so she didn't have to. "Can she have that information, boss?" "Give her anything she needs that doesn't violate a law," he said, covering his ass. Since he wouldn't have known which laws we might be breaking and since she didn't either, this meant yes.

She grunted and then looked up. "I can email them to you. Is there anything else you need before you leave the office?" I looked at her for a moment and thought how her words were not in themselves intensely hateful; it was more the way they were projected. My mother had a similar power, a way to say something that sounded nice enough till you rolled it around in your head and realized that it wasn't. My mother still said nice things to me, like, "Well, since you're a lady of leisure you can come help me." Or, "Are you still working for Harry?" Because obviously my job was not real. I was making it up and just sitting around spending my days doing nothing. I almost wanted to take photos of all the people I'd spoken to so far today trying to get information, and text it to my mom with the caption, "See? I am not just avoiding you. I am busy." But it didn't matter. She wouldn't believe me.

"No, thank you," I said, smiling my biggest smile at Amanda. Because no matter how deeply she wanted me dead, it didn't matter. If she had met me during middle school she would have made me cry. I just wasn't someone who could be hurt by her type anymore.

Maria gives me the Lowdown on the Evicted

I drove to Maria's office with the light air of someone who knows that the worst part of their day is behind them and that the rest of the day is a downhill slide to sleep.

Maria had texted me and told me she was in the office alone, so I'd texted her back asking for her Starbucks order. I'd hit the drive-through and brought her a large (because I'm not about to start using Starbucks' sizes. If I did that it might roll into different things. Like that guy I dated in senior year in high school. I could refer to him as a tall. In the Starbucks definition it would mean he was unsatisfyingly small in every way) cold brew with vanilla cream, which turned out to have whipped cream on top. Meanwhile, I got myself a triple-shot latte. I'd already reached my max on caffeine but who was counting?

Maria had the door propped open and the cool breeze was moving into the office. It felt almost lovely. I wondered what would happen if Amanda opened her door at work. Would the sun come in, touch her complexion, and she'd burst into flame?

Maria pulled a chair up next to her for me. "So what can I do to help you?""Well," I said, opening my phone and my notes. "The first thing I was hoping for was a list of evicted tenants over the last six months or so. I heard that some people were evicted from the Virgil apartment building. I was wondering if you could tell me anything about them.""Oh, them... I don't know if I have any up-to-date information, but I can look.""Do you guys evict a lot of people?""Not too many. Maybe like ten different apartments in the last year, and a couple of businesses.""Businesses?""Yes. Actually, the laundromat that burned—that used to belong to a man called Wasserman, but he got behind in the rent, and let it go to hell, and Mrs. Arkbari evicted him.""Oh wow.""Yeah. The rumor is he had a coke problem and he stopped fixing the machines and let it all run down. Then the city told him that he had to start water reclamation and clean the discharge water, and he stopped paying rent. It's a commercial property so Mrs. Arkbari gave him a three-day notice to pay or quit, and he didn't pay, so she changed the locks.""Three days... What the hell? That was his business. He had to be pissed."

"That's standard with a commercial property. Actually, he brought in a truck and cleared out the newer washers and dryers and left us with a pile of broken-down machines and a bill to the city."

"When was this?" I said, grabbing out my notepad, because it seemed to me like coked-up laundromat owner needed to go on the list of possible suspects. I mean, it was more likely that it was him than Phil, right? Right?

"Oh, about two years ago. I'll find the date. Mrs. Arkbari decided to just spend the money on the equipment and keep the business running since it was a low-touch business."

"Two years ago?" I sighed. I could be wrong but my hypothesis was that whoever did this was angry, and angry didn't last two years. Six months maybe, but not two years.

"Is it normal for Mrs. A to take over a business?"

"No, not at all."

"Is it common knowledge that she owns this business?"

"No," said Maria.

"It's not in public records?

"I don't think so," said Maria.

"How about the tenants at the apartments? What can you tell me about that?"

"Oh, that was bad," said Maria. "They had lived there a really long time, and then the mom, Luisa, lost her job—because she was the housekeeper to this old lady who went into a home—and her sons... well, Ronaldo was in school and she wanted to keep him in school so he could do something better, but he wasn't making any money, and her other son... he was unemployed and looking for a job but he couldn't find one, and her daughter had just had the baby, so it was hard."

"So they ended up homeless on the streets of LA?" "Well, the oldest son—his girlfriend let them move in with her family temporarily." "You seem to know quite a lot about them." "Well, it just wasn't fair, you know? So I talked to the cleaners who clean our offices here and I got Luisa a job with them. And her oldest son is working with my brother. He runs a home help service for older people. And Ronaldo just got accepted into UCLA for a degree in engineering. So they are going to be ok." I turned to look at Maria. She really was an angel. "Let me guess. You also found them somewhere else to live?"

"Oh yes." She bit her lip and looked ashamed. "You can't tell Mrs. Arkbari."

"Promise."

"Mrs. Arkbari has a different apartment building closer to their new jobs and I sort of let them move in for the same rent they were paying on the old place. I just put the lease in the name of Ronaldo this time. And if they get into any trouble paying the rent, they can come talk to me."

"Aren't you afraid you're going to end up getting screwed? What if they don't pay and now you have to pay out of your own pocket?"

"It's possible," smiled Maria. "But I have enough. I can afford to help where I can."

Well, that was that. The two evicted tenants most likely to burn the places down actually had no real reason to do so. Maybe there were other evictions.

"You haven't helped any of the other evicted people, have you?"

"No," said Maria. "But this was a special case. I was there looking at the property repairs that day with Mrs. Arkbari and I started talking to Ronaldo. He was there and he was angry, so I pulled him aside and started to talk to him in Spanish about what the problem was. And I just couldn't do nothing."

It seemed silly to argue with her that she could have done nothing. That most people would have done nothing, that she had no real possibility of this doing anything but biting her in the ass. If Mrs. Arkbari found out, Maria could lose her job. If Luisa and Ronaldo didn't make the rent, Maria would need to pay it.

I wanted to hug Maria and also slap her. How could she put herself into this much potential trauma?

"So how many more people has Mrs. Arkbari evicted in the last six months?" I said, and Maria pulled up a list. Most of them lived too far away for me to consider that they would go to Hollywood to burn down two buildings. Two of them were close. In Silverlake, Mrs.

Arkbari had apparently evicted a young man called Jordan Sproutley, and in Koreatown she'd evicted a family named Li.

I could probably track down Jordan Sproutley but the idea of trying to find a family named Li somewhere in Los Angeles seemed impossible. Still, I wrote down the details, such as they were, social security numbers, phone numbers, occupations.

I had two more possible suspects who weren't Phil.

I wasn't sure if that made me happier or sadder.

"You said you and Mrs. Arkbari went to the apartment while it was being repaired," I said. "Did you also go to the laundromat?"

"I didn't," said Maria, "not that time. It was pretty simple—just some blocked drain lines that had to be replaced. Mrs. Arkbari might have gone. I'm not sure but I can check her calendar."

Maria pulled up a calendar on her screen. She typed in the property address and the calendar filtered until it was only things concerning that property. Repair dates, property tax billing dates, tenant entrance and exit dates. She zeroed in on the dates for the plumbing repair at the laundromat, then clicked a different button to show Mrs. A's schedule.

"Yes, it looks like she went to the property during that repair," said Maria.

So Phil had definitely lied, or maybe accidentally been confused. Maria and Mrs. Arkbari had come to the apartment building. Maria had never been to the laundromat but Mrs. Arkbari had. Why had Phil lied?

All the Loose Ends

I spent the next day going through my notes and wishing I was both better organized and had neater writing. What was that word I'd written in the side about Maria? Why did I care anyway? Maria wasn't the arsonist. I was sure of very little but I was sure of that.

I did a quick Google of Jordan Sproutley and found his Instagram page. He'd apparently moved back into his mom's house in Houston and was working at an IHoP. So he wasn't guilty of the arsons no matter what other food service atrocities he may be liable for.

I started a credit check on the social security number and name listed on the Li family's rental application. At least Mr. Li had moved to Bakersfield, where it looked like he was now the proud owner of a small business. I was happy for him, and also happy to cross all the Lis off the list, because no one was going to drive from Bakersfield for money, let alone revenge.

Wasserman, the former owner of the laundromat, was strangely absent in all social media, and Google didn't give me anything either. I couldn't prove that he wasn't the arsonist returning after two years to burn down his building but it seemed unlikely that he would know that Mrs. Arkbari also owned a building nearby or that after two years he would all of a sudden care enough to threaten her and burn her shit down.

The worst thing about spending time working on a computer is that your phone beeps and then you realize that you haven't renewed your auto insurance and that the registration to your car is about to run out and that you need to check your bank balance to see if you can afford to renew your auto insurance. Well, maybe this is just me. But I find myself bouncing about, and less gets completed than I would have thought possible.

It was at this point I realized I'd never finished going through all the credit reports of everyone working at Bronson Construction. Not that I needed to go through everyone's credit reports. Just those guys I'd met and talked to. So I'd already seen Amanda's and Phil's.

I still needed to look at Rob, Freddie, Armando, Steve, Peet and Mario. Rob had the credit report I expected. It was almost blank—just a couple of credit cards that were in his name and his mother's name and a car payment which he'd always paid on time (or his mother had).

Freddie's credit score was awful. Truly awful. Looked like he'd been unemployed for a while, living on credit cards, and had never managed to pay off what he owed. I felt for him. But a 514 credit score didn't make you an arsonist, just someone who needed steadier work.

Armando's credit score was minimal too, but because he'd never gotten a credit card. Or bought anything he hadn't paid for in cash.

Steve's credit score was better than my mom's. (Yes, I'd pulled my mother's credit report. If she stopped paying her bills, I wanted to know so I could find out if there was a problem I needed to solve.) He had $40,000 in available credit and a car he'd paid off.

Peet's credit report was almost as empty as Armando's. He'd had nothing until about two years ago when there were inquiries for him to rent an apartment. He had a small Home Depot credit card with a $1000 credit line on it. It looked like he used it to buy tools and paid it off every month. Nothing too strange.

Mario's credit report looked like he was on the verge of bankruptcy. Debts to every store, every bank, every credit card company. He definitely had never left home without a credit card in his pocket. It was not a pretty picture. He'd even done one of those debt consolation loans and then run all the cards up again. It still didn't make him an arsonist but I was glad I wasn't dating him.

I called Speedy Spark Electrical where Macy answered the phone. Macy seemed like she could be Amanda's sister. "Hi. I was given your name by Amanda at Bronson Construction. Two properties have been burned in Hollywood and they were both serviced by your company last month. I was wondering if I could get the names of the electricians who went out to the jobs."

"I am not authorized to give out that kind of information to people who call us."

"I am not asking for their personal details."

"Any information you wish to obtain, please present the court order obliging us to open our files."

"Thanks so much," I said, the bile rising in my mouth. "If I need to I will."

"You're welcome," said Macy.

The line went dead in my hand and I placed the phone very carefully down on the table and walked away for a minute before I did the thing I really wanted to do, which was throw the phone across the entire room and through the window.

I came back to the desk and back to the endless computer searching. I missed the idea of going to talk to humans. It wouldn't have been faster, but there was a risk I would have strangled Macy in person.

Facebook and NextDoor for Mrs. A contained nothing I hadn't heard about already. The "hateful" posts about Israel had all been removed by Maria. The NextDoor video post of the young man standing by his constipated poodle while it strained outside Mrs. A's house was almost funny.

I put the young man's name on my suspects' list. Joesph Albright and his poor constipated puppy were now on the list but not high up.

I decided to find out what was in the public records. There was no record that Mrs. A owned the laundromat. The LLC that owned the laundromat did not have to declare who owned it, and it wasn't searchable through the Secretary of State.

To that degree, it wasn't really easy to find out who owned the properties owned by Mrs. A either. If you searched for the properties, you could find what entity owned a property, but if that entity was a corporation or a trust, then finding out who were the humans behind that entity was very difficult.

A little Googling and the County Clerk and Tax Assessor's office both led me to the corporation that owned these properties. But unless you knew that Mrs. A and her brother Aaron owned the corporation, you would never know. No one would ever really know that Mrs. A owned three hundred properties. Even this corporation only owned part of the real estate portfolio. The rest was owned by a different incorporated trust.

I pulled up the payroll reports Amanda had given me. I could read everything for the last few months and possibly kill myself trying, or I could just check what dates they were working on Mrs. A's laundromat or the apartment in Hollywood.

I found the dates and it looked like everyone was at work. Armando was not off work with COVID during this repair. So everyone was still on the list. I'd worked all day, chased my tail, checked my bank account balance, and managed to move some money so I wasn't bouncing anything. And that was the only thing I'd done all day that seemed useful at all.

Instead of Sleeping, I Solve the Case

I was filled with that deep, jagged exhaustion. The kind that won't let you sleep. It keeps you awake thinking back on all your failures and spinning the wheels in your head again and again until all you have is spinning anxiety. And a desire for sleep. If I thought it would help I would pray for sleep. But I knew what would fix it easily enough. I just wasn't ready to call the one-night stand and make it a two-night stand. That seemed like a commitment, and God knows I wasn't ready for a commitment. Especially not with whatever his name was. He was only ever meant to be a one-night stand.

My tired brain swirled all the problems of this case. There was no suspect. Not one, not two, not six. But hundreds—hundreds of suspects. Thousands of possible suspects. All of them without a clear motive, but all of them with possibly a motive. Who knew what this old lady had done to annoy somebody at some point? And now there were two buildings burnt to the ground. And no one had been hurt.

I was beginning to hope that a third building would burn. On schedule, tomorrow. So that I would possibly have more leads. Maybe not even a whole building. Just a third of a building, preferably something with no one in it. If one could just burn to the ground and provide me with enough leads to narrow this down from several million people to maybe only fifty. Because otherwise there was nothing to go on. And I wanted to sleep. But I also wanted that extra building to burn. Wanted to get that call somehow. Despite the best security, despite the police being on guard, despite everything, I wanted to hear that yet another building Mrs. Arkbari owned had turned to nothing but ash and dust.

I was doom-scrolling Instagram and pretending to sleep when Harry called. "Third building has burned."

"Well, good evening to you too, Harry." I turned the light on and groaned. "It's late. I was trying to be asleep. Surely it could wait till tomorrow."

"There's a body."

"Someone was killed in the fire?" I said, now feeling incredibly guilty for spending time in my bed checking out the posts of people I don't really care about rather than solving the arson already. Guilty for wanting another building to burn. Not that I knew how to solve the arson. Not that I hadn't gone over all my notes before I jumped in the shower to help me sleep. Not that I wasn't waiting to get more information during business hours. But damn it, if I had caused someone's death by not being good enough, by not being fast enough, by not working hard enough, well, I may really suck.

"Nope, not killed in the fire," said Harry, and I sighed in relief. "Found the body after the fire was out."

"So nothing we could have done?"

"Mrs. Arkbari is sure we could have. The arson inspector will meet you on-site at seven a.m., and then Mrs. Arkbari wants a briefing in her office at nine."

"So you just called to tell me that I am not getting any sleep?"

"Of course you are getting sleep. You have about four hours to do it. The next fire location is downtown in the Art District. I will text you the address. Of course, you don't need to sleep. You could just work all night and be dazed and confused and grumpy. I don't think we want to see you grumpy."

"Goodnight, Harry."

"Goodnight, Sophie. Be on time!"

"Go to hell, Harry."

"Hell doesn't want me back." I chuckled and heard Tiny Tim growling at the sound of my voice. "Sleep well, girlie. Tomorrow is going to be a day of it."

I would never have called Harry sexist or racist, although he most assuredly was. It was more a question of what he was not. Prejudiced against women or people of color he definitely was but it wasn't that he hated any one race or sex. More that he distrusted and had no faith in humanity, and to that degree didn't trust women or men and people of any color. It was a fact Harry just generally disliked humanity and everyone in it. He wasn't actually prejudiced against any one person or group. He genuinely disliked the entire human race, including himself.

While he found humanity in general lacking, the only thing he did not think was lacking was Tiny Tim, his Chihuahua.

Tiny Tim hated humanity almost as much as Harry did and would attack anybody at any time. I think that's why Harry liked me. Because I didn't run away from Tiny Tim. Because there's something about a charging Chihuahua that really makes you want to get some distance. I mean, a German shepherd can growl and snarl and have big teeth, but there's just something about a little psychotic Chihuahua with his eyes bulging, barely able to breathe, coughing and shaking in fury, with all of its teeth showing, that just makes your worst nightmares come true.

I had to laugh that even hearing my voice on the phone could set Tiny Tim off.

The worst thing about knowing you need to sleep because you have to get up early is that the minute you tell yourself to sleep it is the last thing you can do. So I got up and started reading through all the invoices I had copied at Amanda's office again.

I started lining them up. Not by property this time but by date. Both properties had had the plumber visit. The plumber came to the first property in January and the second property in March. The first occasion was a leaking gas line in the apartment complex, and in the laundromat the plumber had to fix a water recycling system. Both properties had also had an electrician visit. Both visits had been in July. The air conditioners had overloaded the circuit board at the apartment building and they had to put in a larger amp fuse box. In the laundromat a small electrical fire had set off fire alarms and the electrician had been out on an emergency basis to rewire two machines.

Apart from that, Amanda had invoiced out a lot of standard maintenance for the apartment building. Three tenants had changed so there were painting and recarpeting invoices. One kitchen had been upgraded. And then there were five or six broken windows and one busted lock. Apparently one tenant had repeatedly locked her boyfriend out and he'd thought the best solution was to kick down the door.

In the file was the police report and the photos for the insurance company. I suspected that the police knew the building well. It was obviously the kind of apartment that was cheap. Cheap to the point where people who could live anywhere better would. Cheap to the point where it was the last apartment before you started living in your car. Still expensive compared to housing in other places in the world, and because of this it was apartments like this where most of the young children grew up in Los Angeles.

I was lucky. I got to grow up in the suburbs, with good schools and safe streets. The child who had lost their tricycle in the fire was growing up on a street filled with traffic, and pollution, and police car sirens. They wouldn't have even been allowed onto the sidewalk outside the apartment because it would be filled with homeless people, human urine and trash. It would have been too unsafe to even leave the balcony that joined one apartment to the other. The balcony that joined all the small apartments to the next so one sound could vibrate around. I'd rented an apartment like that when I was younger, when I first moved out, an apartment where you locked the doors behind you every night and prayed that the neighbor's fight was going to end so you could sleep. Where you prayed that when the screaming and pounding stopped next door the silence wasn't the sign that someone was dead.

The maintenance bills showed exactly the type of place this was. Repairing a hole in the wall there, putting a new door in to replace a broken one. Fixing the washing machine because it had been over-loaded and someone had broken the coin-operated system so it ran for free.

Laundry, I thought, my mind running. Both fires had started in the laundry. The other specialist that had come to both properties was a washer repair company. I lined up the two invoices. A Plus Laundry Repair had been on-site both properties this month, August. I looked at the bills from A Plus Laundry Repair. It looked like the same signature. The same technician had come to both buildings. I smiled. It was the laundry guy. It had to be the laundry guy.

I climbed back into bed, leaving the bills strewn over my bedroom floor. I plugged in my phone, turned off my light, and slept the tranquil sleep of someone who has solved the problem. Until three and a half hours later when my phone screamed out an alarm. I woke up looking over the mess I had made and smiled, knowing I'd worked out the impossible problem. The fires were started by the laundry repair guy.

Burnt Body Wall Cavity is not the Name of a Rock Band

I threw myself and a large coffee in the car. The only thing nice about driving in LA in the morning traffic is that you go so slow you really don't have to worry about having an accident, because how much damage can an accident cause at seven miles per hour? It was early, so the full traffic jam hadn't formed yet. Later, knowing Los Angeles traffic, the speed would be more like three miles an hour. I looked over at my GPS. The hard part was going to be finding somewhere to park. I finally found a metered spot a block or two away and walked to the next arson site. It was early and homeless people lay sleeping still in the corners of the bus stops and stores which had not yet opened. Reggie, my formerly homeless friend, had explained to me that the hard part about being homeless was that you couldn't sleep. That at any moment you might not be safe, so you never slept deeply or well, and it was safer to sleep in the day and be awake in the night.

I'd never thought about it, but it made sense. If I couldn't lock the door I'd never sleep.

I'd talked to Reggie a few nights ago. He and Marv had moved into a house and were running it as a halfway house for people who wanted to get back into society. It was nice to know I'd managed to do something right, at least for them.

I remember when the last mayor was elected she talked about how she was going to sort out the homeless situation in Los Angeles, but ever since the pandemic it's been worse than ever. It feels helpless. I feel helpless. I understand when there are so many people living on the street why some people feel threatened. I understand why it's easier to look the other way, to ignore the problem. But it's not a problem. A problem is flies in the backyard. A problem is a mouse infestation. This is not a problem. These are people, living out their lives in the public places of the city. It makes me feel sad and angry and helpless.

I could smell the building before I turned the corner. It was on 4th Street, at Alameda, in an area that is now called the Arts District but is right next door to an area that has always been called Skid Row. Homelessness is not a new thing in Skid Row, it's been the mainstay of the area for about a hundred years. The Great Depression started the skid downwards. The only thing that is different is that the city can't contain the "problem" anymore into the fifty-city-block radius where it used to be.

The whole building was black and charred. The sign was barely visible above the blown-out windows. "Wholesale Smoke: Cigarettes and Cigars." The humorous irony was apparently lost on my friend Jeff Delmonico—Arson Investigator. He stood in front with a helmet on and a helmet in his hand for me.

"Thank you for meeting me," I said. "We may have gotten off on the wrong foot last time..." I started the apology, waiting for him to chime in and knowing he wouldn't. Apologizing is what women do, not men. "So I just wanted to apologize and thank you for showing me the building."

"Ok," he grunted, not apologizing back. Not understanding that when I thanked him for showing me the building I was really just thanking him for doing his job. I decided I had said enough and I wasn't going to apologize or even be polite because at this point he'd probably take it as a come-on and decide I wanted him. Men can get the wrong end of the stick so easily.

The building hadn't been boarded up yet. And the police were moving in and out. The windows and doors had blown out. The building had burned almost completely. Plumbing lines hung from the ceiling. Under my feet crunched the remains of burned cases of cigarettes. Firemen had cut holes in the roof to put the fire out and the whole building felt like it was minutes away from collapsing. I was hoping this was just my impression. I guessed if it had really been that close to collapse they wouldn't have had so many cops inside taking pictures and collecting evidence. "Where did the fire start?" I asked.

"In the bathroom."

"Not the laundry washer?"

"No laundry or washer on-site, just an office, a storeroom, and a toilet."

Damn, that was my fevered solution from two in the morning all shot to hell. I had been following him eyes down, making sure I didn't trip over anything.

Then he said, "Here is the body."

I looked up, surprised to see a skeleton with its arms clawing out. It was sitting, as if it had slid down against the wall. I didn't know if it had fallen out of the wall, or just been placed against the wall when it burned. It was nothing but bone-white bones. Ok, redundant, but the bones were clean, white, with no sign of flesh. Like they were props from an old spaghetti Western film when the bones are found crawling their way to a watering hole which had just dried up.

I looked over at Jeff. He was smiling. He'd wanted to shock me. The only reason he'd agreed to show me around this site today while it was still an active investigation was because he wanted to freak me out. I'd seen that face too many times when I was a kid. Circ and his brothers had always tried to get a rise out of the girl next door. He really should have tried that trick when I was younger. The 32-year-old version of me was a little more scared of my mother living to a hundred than I was of a corpse.

"Ok, I will ask forensics for information about that. What else can you tell me about the fire? Was it the same accelerant?"

"It looks like it," he said, a little disappointed.

"How do you know?"

"Well, the burn pattern is the same, and preliminary chem tests say gasoline. We'll know for sure when I get back to the lab."

"Ok, thanks."

"Why else do you think you are here?" he said. "If it wasn't the same arsonist I wouldn't have called your boss."

"The building seems to have burned faster than the last one," I said, ignoring his pouting. "I thought commercial buildings burned slower."

"Yes, in general. But this one was filled with fuel. Cigarettes are by nature designed to burn. And there was $100,000's worth of cigars and cigarettes in the storeroom. So this place went up like a tinder box."

There Might be More Bodies we Missed

"Or a wooden ashtray," I said, and he looked at me as if I had suddenly grown three sixes on my forehead.

As my dad would say, screw 'em if they can't take a joke. I miss my dad. It seems like he's been gone forever, yet sometimes I feel like he was just in the room with me. Telling me some dirty joke he'd heard that he didn't think was inappropriate to repeat to your teenage daughter. Or taking me with him to the garage to sit on the piece of wood he was cutting, or help hold the light while he worked on the truck's engine. I think my happiest place as a child was in the safety of the garage, helping Dad, getting a soda that he kept for me out of the garage fridge, being treated like I was important and not just a nuisance who had left the toothpaste open again to drip onto the sink.

It just never occurred to me that one day he wouldn't be there. That one day the one man I loved would be gone, and that feeling of safety would go with him.

"How long did it take the building to burn?" I asked, not really caring because, honestly, it didn't change my life at all. What difference did it make to me if it took twenty minutes or seventy-four hours? My job was to find the guy who started it, not critique him on his work.

"We think the fire started at about ten last night. It was small but the heat built and then it roared through everything. Firemen finally got the blaze abated at one a.m."

"So they were working for a long time," I said, looking around the ruins of the building, the metal studs now exposed, the drywall gone, the ceiling making me glad I had a hard hat on. The area where the body had been found was near the office so it must have been one of the first to burn.

Forensics had finished taking photos and were pulling the body out of the wall cavity where it had been squeezed between the studs. I sure hoped the poor bastard had gone into the wall dead.

"They were lucky this time. They got it before it spread. Only this building was destroyed. There was minor damage at five other buildings."

"Does it generally take that long to control a fire this size?," I said.

"There were one hundred and seventy men fighting the fire," he said, feeling the need to justify exactly how much work had gone into it. The funny thing is, I was sure he meant that there were exactly one hundred and seventy men—not firemen, not fire people, but men. After all, who'd actually seen or heard of a firewoman?

"That's a lot," I said.

"Fire like this, if it gets out of control the whole Downtown is in danger." He put his hands on his hips as he said this to reinforce his mansplaining and also to remind me that he was a douche no matter how well he filled out his khakis.

"What do we know about the body?" I asked.

"Not my department," he answered.

"Do you think that the arsonist burned the place to destroy the body and the evidence of a murder?"

"I am sure of it," he said. "We are going to be looking for human remains in the first two fires to see if this was the real reason for the arsons."

"But wouldn't the arsonist start all the fires at the location in the building where the bodies actually were if that was the case?"

He gave me one of those 'girl, you so stupid' stares and stared to mansplain again. "Obviously, the arsonist started the fires in the area where he was least likely to be seen. He also started the fires at times when the buildings should not have been occupied. What we don't know is how the arsonist got into this building. The doors were locked. So we think he may have broken in the back door. It is hard to know at this point because the door was destroyed."

"So you think he got in quick and got out?"

"The accelerant was not spread widely in any of the fires. Just at the source. So yes, it is my considered opinion that he came in, doused the accelerant, threw the igniter and then quickly exited the building."

"So you think it was a quick in-and-out job," I said, momentarily thinking that Harry would describe my recent dating life in much the same way.

"Yes. It had to be."

"So how did he put the body in the wall?" I asked.

"The body had to have been in the wall before the fire," said the expert.

"Ok," I said.

Then I thought, if the body was already in the wall, how do we know for sure that the murderer and the arsonist are the same person? This body was inside the wall. We don't know how long it had been inside the wall. Since the owner of the cigarette shop never said, "Hey, by the way, there's a person who's dead sticking out my wall," I thought we could safely assume that the drywall covered them and no one knew they were there. Either that or the guy who owned the cigarette shop—I'm being sexist; maybe a woman owned the cigarette shop but really, what's the odds of that—so the guy who owned the cigarette shop... maybe he killed his wife, stuck her in the wall, then covered the place with boxes and boxes of stock so no one knew.

Maybe there was a smell. Maybe people thought it was rats. Maybe you couldn't smell anything over a couple thousand menthols and cigars.

Where I wish I was still a Police Detective

I could see that Jeff had had more than enough of me, and it wasn't like the feeling wasn't mutual. So I wandered off to see if I could talk to the police involved.

I knew enough to know I wouldn't find the detective in charge of the investigation standing here in the rubble smelling the remains of a million cigarettes or waiting for the roof to cave in on them. And I'd had enough of both myself. I needed to let Jeff do his job and take some samples back to the lab to see what kind of accelerant was used. I walked out into the sunlight, and only as I did I realized that I'd been holding my breath.

I looked at my hands and my skin was coated in fine black ash. Even though the fire was out, it was still falling. I had to wonder how much this would contribute to my death and whether breathing LA air wasn't already a life-shortening experience.

The detective was at the edge of the perimeter. He was about fifty, with a belly that had enjoyed a lot of Sunday football as a spectator.

You knew he was the detective by his cheap suit and the way the uniformed cops swarmed around him like bees reporting back to the queen.

I walked up to him, my dirty hand out, as soon as there was a break in the swarm. "I'm Sophie Drake, private investigator."

"Working for the insurance company?" he said, waving my hand away.

"No," I said. "The owner of the property engaged our services after the second fire."

"Oh," he said. "A civilian shouldn't be here. You can contact the office to see if there is any public information we can give you."

"Thank you, sir. With whom exactly should I speak?"

"Call the switchboard. They can sort you out."

"And what is your name, sir?" I said, the corner of my mouth twitching, because I had reached that point in my life where if I was using the word *sir*, it was a direct replacement for *fuckface*. The more I used *sir* the angrier I was getting.

"Detective Lacinku," he said, turning his back to me and going back to talking to his guys. I walked over to the forensics team.

It was a man and a woman. They had loaded the remains into their vehicle. The man was standing at the side of the van smoking a cigarette and the woman was sitting in the passenger's seat with the door open, writing notes on her laptop. I walked up to her.

"Hi. I was just speaking to the detective and he said I should talk to you guys directly."

"How can I help you?" The woman looked up with that slightly perplexed look that people who need strong glasses have. She'd been staring at the screen with her glasses pushed up on her forehead. She pulled them down to see me and her face relaxed as she focused.

"Hi. My name is Sophie Drake. I work for the owner of the building. This is the third building she owns that has been torched and I was hired to help solve the arsons."

"There weren't any corpses in the first two buildings?"

"No. At least not that we know of."

"That's probably why I haven't heard of them."

I smiled. "Exactly. I was hoping that I could call you when you have more information about the corpse?"

"It will take a few days, at least."

"Well, I'm Sophie. What's your name?"

"Daisy."

"Daisy, I hope you don't mind if I give you a call in a day or two."

She smiled. "Nope. I'll help if I can."

Mike's Way Plumbing and I Catch a Sandwich

Since I'd gotten the appointment with Mike's Way Plumbing I told Harry I wouldn't be able to meet with Mrs. A. He could deal with her judgemental attitude without me. I'm sure she would be super happy that we hadn't solved the case yet.

When I was younger, I realized that there were only actually two types of boys. Annoying ones and forgettable ones. Later, as I got older, there were still only two kinds of boys. Kissable ones and unkissable ones. And later only two kinds of men, fuckable ones and unfuckable ones. Mike was definitely in the non-fuckable variety. Pasty skin and the body of a garden gnome. He was the kind who generally hit on me. Today was not going to break that pattern.

"Well," he said, licking his lower lip with a large fleshy tongue. "Phil told me you'd be calling, and normally I'm out on a job, you know, but it was slow enough today to send the boys out."

"And who are the boys, Mr. Way?"

"Call me Mike."

"And who are the boys, sir?" I said.

He didn't seem to notice the "sir." Troll-like men only manage to reproduce because they are completely ignorant of their troll-like qualities. Phil had told me that Mike was a nice guy, a friend of his even, and I could only imagine that he was much different with men than he was with women. This was not the first time I'd observed something like this, but it didn't make it any easier for me to sit on the chair across from him.

I'd come to the office of Mike's Way Plumbing. It was barely an office—more like a dirty warehouse and place to park the plumbing van at night. The office was wood panel that had been poor quality when it had been installed in 1952, and the desk was one of those metal ones you remember used to be in institutions, until even institutions decided they didn't want them anymore. I was sitting on a green office chair made of steel and vinyl, and whereas I was sure that some antique dealer would quite happily tell me what year it was made and rave on about how mid-century modern furniture was so collectable, all I could think was that the padding had crapped out forty years before and it was gross and sticky.

When I had called, Mike had told me he'd be in the office the rest of the day, so I figured I should cross him and his "boys" off the list.

"The boys are my son, little Mikey, and our other plumber, Jack."

Names are something I have very strong opinions about. Growing up with Circus gave me a solid grounding on how much damage the wrong name could do. And I consider poor naming choices to be a sign of narcissism and abuse. I also consider calling someone Junior or your own name is a sure sign of mental deficiency and generally only seen in weak men who need a masculine ego trip. A grown man should not have to live under the shadow of his father with a name that is nothing but a diminutive version of Daddy's name. Mikey was not a name for a grown man.

"How old are the boys?" I said, asking because perhaps the silly, childish name was because little Mikey was still in high school.

"Well, Mikey's going to be 32 this year, and Jack is in his thirties I guess; never asked."

So I had ascertained in the three minutes that I'd been sitting on this ugly, sticky little chair that Mike Way Senior was definitely a narcissist. He may or may not be an arsonist. The two are not necessarily an intersecting group. I could just see my middle-school math teacher, Mrs. Vive, trying to explain it on a Venn diagram drawn with dying whiteboard markers. "This, children, is a group of toys owned by boys. This is a group of toys owned by girls. Some toys are owned by both boys and girls." At which point the class smart-ass, Adam, asked, "What about the toys Mommy has in the drawer next to the bed? The ones owned by grownups?"

"So how long have you been a plumber, Mike?"

"Oh, I've had this business for about 30 years. Started when little Mikey was a baby."

"And how many of Mrs. Arkbari's buildings do you do repairs on?"

"I have no idea. We don't work for her, we work for Bronson Construction. I didn't even realize that the laundromat and the apartment building were both owned by one person until Phil called me to see if I could talk to you."

"You don't get told whose buildings they are?" I said, my head tipping to one side slightly.

"No, not at all. I mean, we've been on-site when that Mrs. Arkbari came by. I think she might have come to the laundromat once, but it wasn't like we was introduced. I mean, we were knee-deep in broken sewer lines, and the stench... I heard she was there, or someone was, but we didn't exactly shake hands."

"And your boys, would they have met her?"

"Oh God, no. I mean, I was pretty clean compared to what they were working on. They were waist-deep in—"

"Thanks. I don't actually think I have any more questions." I stood up, peeling myself off the sticky vintage chair.

He shot up. "Oh, please don't go so soon. I can make you a coffee or a tea or—"

"No, thanks," I said, looking over at his aged Keurig machine and powdered creamer on top of his rusty file cabinet. "I'm good, thanks."

I walked towards the door and he followed right behind me. "Sure you don't want to stay and see the boys?"

"Nope, think I'm good, thanks." I started to walk out to the front door through the warehouse and he followed me. I opened the door to the daylight and I turned to see him, in all his pitiful loneliness. He looked sad as an ugly puppy.

"Ok, well, if you think of anything you'd like to know... I'd just like to help."

I turned back on him. "Phil says you and he go flying together."

"Oh yes. Phil lets me go with him a couple of times a month. Phil owns a plane."

Phil hadn't told me he owned his own plane. What else wasn't Phil telling me?

"Phil's a great guy, you know, always does what he thinks is right. A real man's man."

"How long have you known Phil?" I asked.

"Maybe twenty-five years," said Mike. "We're both bachelors, you know. But he had a girlfriend a couple years ago, and I thought that was it, I thought we'd have to stop hanging out. But then one day she just vanished, and he and I had time to go bowling and just hanging out, you know. It's been hard ever since my wife left. Mikey was about fifteen and one day his mom just takes off. Phil was there for us. Told us not to worry, that we were better off without her. Phil is my best friend, you know."

I nodded. Phil might be his best friend but right now Phil was my lead suspect and I had to wonder if the body in the walls wasn't Phil's last girlfriend. Or Mike's wife.

I pulled my business card out of my purse and Mike clutched at it. "If you think of anything strange you've seen at either of the properties that burned, give me a call.""Sure," he said, his fleshy tongue going out to lick his lips again. I swallowed down my bile and walked out to my car.

I did not like Mike. But I believed him. He worked for Bronson Construction, not Mrs. Arkbari.

So who did that really leave in my suspect pool?

Phil, because he had access to the fuel. And maybe because his girlfriend, who had just disappeared, had just burnt to death in a cigarette warehouse. But what was his motive? I wanted to know he had a solid reason for torching the places. Unless they found bodies in the first two properties, I could not assume that the murders and the arsons were committed by the same person.

Then there was Phil's crew. Who mostly claimed not to know Mrs. A. Except that they did. They had all met her at one time or another at one of her properties. I couldn't rule out any of them yet, so Armando, Freddie, Mario, Rob, Steve and Peet.

The evicted tenants weren't suspects. Maria had made sure they were happy. What about Maria herself? How could anybody stay that nice when they were dealing with such a demanding shrew day in and day out? I mean, I thought she was way too nice, but then Ted Bundy's victims had all thought he was a swell guy too until he started to rape and kill them. You couldn't just base everything on looks. I needed to put Amanda back on the list too. I'd crossed her off too soon, but she had access to all the records. Someone needed to know what properties Mrs. A owned. Who had access to the records? Whoever had access to the records could have lit the fires. And Mike's Way and by extension Sparks Electrical didn't have access to the records. Like Mike had said, the client they worked for wasn't Mrs. A. It was the construction company.

I'd been looking at this all wrong. There weren't a million suspects. There were twenty, and they all worked for Mrs. Arkbari or for Bronson Construction. I needed to know if anyone else worked for Mrs. Arkbari. I needed to investigate Veronica and Frederick. And I needed to dig into the lives and personalities of the men over at Bronson Construction. Talking to them in brief had only told me what they looked like, but if I was going to find Phil innocent I needed to find another viable suspect, and right now I didn't have one.

I drove over to Jersey Mike's to pick up a sandwich and headed back to the office. I needed to run all the suspects past Harry and see if in between my garbled notes he could see a pattern or a suspect because right now, all I could see was that the nicest guy I'd met in a long time was probably an arsonist, and maybe also a killer.

I was on my way to see my mother this weekend and all she'd ask about was my dating life, and yes, I'd met a lot of men this week, but none of them had actually proven themselves worthy of mentioning to my mother. And as she keeps telling me, "You aren't getting any younger, dear." As if adding *dear* to the end of that sentence actually makes it a nice phrase. And then she tries to set me up. I was really scared that this weekend was another setup, that she'd found some man who she thought could father my children and make her the grandmother she so desperately longed to be.

If disappointing my mother were my objective, there was at least one way that I was winning this weekend.

I wondered if I told my mom about Phil and told her that he was an arsonist and that he'd murdered his ex-girlfriend if she'd still want me to date him. Still root for him. "Well, honey, you know nobody is perfect. You know you're much too fussy."

I remember the last time we'd had a conversation about my single status. She'd started, "I told you years ago you should have married Circus."

"He's gay, Mom."

"So what, dear? That wouldn't have stopped me when I was younger. He's cute enough and rich. I mean, it would give you legal standing, dear. Right now, you know he could kick you out of that nice little apartment you have and you'd be homeless, dear."

I sighed at the memory. The thought of seeing my mother this weekend was not bringing out the best in me.

Where I Eat Cooked Animal Flesh and Discuss Cooked Human Flesh

B ecause I had effectively managed to piss off arson investigator Jeff Delmonico, I had to get Harry to call his boss to find out the information we were looking for. It's strange. Normally people don't totally hate me till after we've had sex, so Jeff was a special case.

But then everything about this was a special case. Jeff had been right at the crime scene. The burn pattern showed pooling of a volatile component, and he'd also been right that this had been a very hot fire. Just like the earlier two fires, this was definitely arson and it looked like 100LL Avgas, 100-octane low-lead aviation fuel, was the accelerant.

I read the report thoroughly. There was only one origin point on the fire. So it was similar to the last two fires. The guy—I was assuming the firebug was a guy—had gotten in and out in probably 10 minutes max. The back door had a code on it and it looked like whoever had come in probably came through the door, which meant they may have known the code.

So now I could cross-reference three different fires by the service calls they had received. This should make it easier, except that what it really meant was that I had to go and visit Amanda again.

I went home to scrub myself down before I went to her office. I called Maria to see if she would put in a good word for me before I went to visit the lioness in her den. I was sure Maria would do as I asked but I was still filled with the kind of apprehension one gets when you have to go visit the principal.

Amanda greeted me cordially, almost warmly, and I felt genuine terror. Carnivores usually only show their teeth before they eat you, and I had to wonder why she was smiling. "Hi, Sophie. Welcome back. If you're going to be here a while, we have a coffee machine in the break room."

I looked over at her, wondering momentarily if it was the same woman.

"Phil tells me that I should give you all the help I can."

Oh, now I understood. Phil had mentioned me. Amanda wasn't being nice to me for her own sake, she was doing it to impress Phil. Now the world made sense. Amanda was always going to be the woman who did things to please men.

"Nice to see you too." I smiled. "I think I know my own way around now. Do you mind if I take some more photos from the file?"

"Not at all. If you need my help with anything, let me know."

I pulled the box out and started pulling receipts for the smoke shop repairs. The main crew had not been out. None of Phil's guys had been to the property for at least two years. So it couldn't be Phil or anyone in his crew, could it? But a plumber and an electrician had been there. It wasn't Mike's Way Plumbing that went to the Hollywood properties. The name for the electrical company seemed the same but that didn't mean they sent the same electrician. And the electrician was there almost four months earlier. How long would someone really hold a grudge? If they were so angry they wanted to burn your shit down, wouldn't they jump on it, not wait four months to find the right kind of lighter fluid?

No laundry repair man, of course. I grimaced at the way that had seemed so logical only the night before. This case was getting the better of me. I was starting to see solutions that were just other threads in the tapestry.

All I had was lots and lots of pieces of thread but I didn't know what the tapestry they were weaving was a picture of, or how many of the threads were from a different tapestry altogether. And now there was a body. How did that fit in? Was the arsonist just covering the crimes he'd already committed by trying to burn the evidence before it was found out?

I didn't know if the body had been in the wall a week, or a month, or a year. For all I knew the body had been dragged into the building, sat up against the wall, the fire had started, and it had just looked like it had come out of the wall.

The arson report said the fire had burned at about 1500 degrees Fahrenheit. At that temperature a body would have been cremated, only the bones remaining, in as little as two hours. Why do I know this? Because these are the fun things I research on my laptop when I am thinking about this case. I mean, I could be spending my spare time watching *10 Things I Hate About You* for the 19th time, or trolling social media for cute dog photos, but instead I am trying to find out what the terms in arson reports mean and how long it takes a human body to go from rare to well done to flesh has melted off and you're left with a skeleton worthy of a high school bio lab. Sometimes I worry that trying to solve crimes makes me less trusting, but then I remember that I never trusted anyone except Circ in the first place.

I haven't seen Circ since our squabble by the pool. I'd probably better check up on him. Make sure he's not so depressed that he's sitting at his computer twenty-four hours a day programming some other app that is going to make him even richer. No one needs the amount of money he already has.

I looked at my watch. It was time for dinner already. It had been a long day. I texted Circ to see if he was home. One of the ways we stay friends is by not assuming that the other one is always available. I live in Circ's pool house and it's been an unspoken rule since I moved in that we don't just wander over.

He texted me back and asked if I wanted to meet at Hank's. Hank's is Circ's favorite hamburger joint, as if any place with a hostess could really be called a joint. He arrived before me and was sitting in his favorite spot at the edge of the outdoor area looking out on all the people walking about in Pacific Palisades going where people went after they left the ridiculously overpriced supermarket Erewhon with one three-hundred-dollar bag of groceries.

I smiled walking up. He really was a good-looking man. "Hey, Circ. What you been up to?"

He smiled back and waved me to sit down. "Trying to help them get the apps updated and secure before the new security protocols come down next year from Apple."

I nodded as if this was something I could visualize. Of course, it wasn't. I just knew that Circ had sold a ton of apps, and that most people had them on their phones. My favorite was his BuyIt app, which actually found what you wanted to buy for the best price and pulled all the coupons to make it as cheap as possible. Circ had sold the apps as he wrote them so he wouldn't have to run any companies.

He didn't want to be Mark Zuckerberg spending all his time running the company of one app. Circ wanted to always make the next new great thing, so he sold every idea. Well, almost sold everything. He still owned 10 percent of each app he had licensed so I suppose that was worth getting out of bed to do a little programming for.

I sat down and pulled out the menu to see if there was anything new I hadn't already had.

"I am sorry we fought," I started.

"I shouldn't talk about who you date." He smirked. "I'm not exactly one to talk."

"I thought you and Vincent showed promise." I remembered the slightly built dark-haired man I'd seen Circ with a few weeks before.

"So did I," said Circ. "But, well... rather not talk about it."

"Fair enough," I said. The waitress was walking towards us. "Time for burgers." I had looked over the whole menu and was going to order what I always ordered, despite the longer list.

"Are you guys ready to order?"

"I'll have a smash burger, sweet potato fries, onion rings and a root beer float," I said.

"Double diamond burger and fries with a coke," said Circ, and handed the waitress his menu.

"You didn't order onion rings, so I am guessing you are planning to steal some of mine," I said, turning to him as the waitress took my menu.

"Steal is such an ugly word. Appropriate, I believe, is the term used in government." He looked at me long and hard for a moment. "How are you doing, Soph? Are you sleeping ok?"

"Is that your not-so-delicate way of telling me I look like shit?"

"You look a bit gray."

"Probably just ash from this morning," I said, grabbing up the glass of water in front of me, realizing I was really tired and dry. "I haven't found the arsonist and they struck again. This time they left a body behind."

"A body? Someone killed in the fire? Man or woman?"

"Not sure. All I saw was a skeleton. Apparently enough heat and you don't have to worry too much about all the messy bits like skin or organs or tissues."

"So they could have been dead before the fire?"

"The theory at this point is that they were killed, placed in the wall of the building, then the building was burned to cover up the murder. They don't even know for sure that this latest fire was set by the same guy. They know the other two fires were because the same accelerant was used.""Oh, he used something unusual?"

"Yeah, Avgas 100LL. It's aviation gasoline with lead. It's used in small planes.""Race cars can use it too. Nice high octane. You go like hell."

"You mean like formula one?""No, like street racers, kind of stuff my brothers would drive. They used to buy it," he said, taking another bite of his burger without letting the idea of a dead human slow him down at all.

He doesn't mention his family as a rule. And as a rule I don't bring them up.

I looked down at my own half burger and the few sweet potato fries that were still left. I had actually seen the body and it didn't look like it had slowed me down either. "Why did they need to burn the building if the body was already hidden in the wall?" asked Circ.

"I had a similar question. I mean, it might have been starting to smell. Or maybe the body wasn't all the way in the wall, just squeezed behind cases against the wall. The police and fire department seem to think the arsonist is also a murderer."

"And what do you think?"

"I'm not convinced. There were no bodies in the first two fires so far as we know. They are going to look for them now that one showed up in this fire. I'm just not sure that because you burn buildings you also off people. They seem like different skill sets. I mean, I park illegally but it doesn't mean I run over pedestrians on the crosswalk."

"So before they found the body, who did you think did it?""Someone who has worked on the buildings. Someone who hates Mrs. A for reasons that are not altogether clear or obvious. I felt like it was personal. I thought for about 10 minutes it was the laundry repair guy but this third fire rules that out—it had no laundry equipment."

Circ nodded to a waitress and our glasses of water were refilled. "Could we also get two lattes?" he asked the waitress. "You want a coffee, right?" he said to me.

"If I ever say no to coffee call the undertaker. Of course I want coffee," I said, thinking I might have to slow down on the root beer float to get the coffee in but it would be worth it.

"I remember when we were kids, you always said you'd get married and have four children."

"Yep. I had the names picked out. Crimson, Amber, Emerald, and Sapphire."

"Well, I hope you've grown out of that at least," Circ said.

"Oh yes. Watching you and your brothers get tormented was sufficient. No unique names for my kids. I will call my kids the standard names of the age, whatever they are. Michael, Katherine, Emma, David... What was your mother thinking calling you guys what she did?"

"I don't know," said Circ. "When we were young she always just said that they were good names and we would grow to appreciate them. But honest to God, how do you appreciate Circus..."

"...or Happy, or Swimming," I said, saying his brothers' names out loud.

"The three of us hated John." He smiled a sad smile.

"What's not to hate? Your oldest brother gets named a real name after your granddad and you and your younger brothers get named after 1st grade spelling bee answers."

"Yeah, I wish I could ask her."

He bit his lip and I felt so bad. Here I was discussing a dead body in a fire when his whole family had been killed in a gas explosion. He'd been on his way back from college for Thanksgiving. The plane was delayed for an East Coast winter storm, and by the time he arrived home late Thanksgiving night the firemen were finished. There was nothing left of his family and of his home, just a burnt-out shell.

"I'm sorry, Circ. I should have guessed fires and bodies would be triggering. I'll talk about something else.""What else are we going to talk about, Soph? Your biological clock and how none of your plans for that family and hubby have panned out yet? Or the fact that Vincent told me he wanted to move in and I wanted it too but when it came to it I couldn't even say yes, and now he's gone..."

Circ pushed his dark sunglasses ever so cooly up his nose but a tear trickled out down the side of his nostril and hit the table.

"You ok?""Apparently not. Let's get the check and go home and watch a movie."

"Yeah, sounds good. Not like I am figuring this damn case out tonight anyway. What do you want to watch? A classic or a horror film?"

Circ has a great theater in his house. The seats are just right—full recliners with lots of room to spread out. And he's had everything covered in patchwork colors so it's got a kind of Willy Wonka vibe, especially with the popcorn and candy dispenser. It may be one of my favorite places. And unless there's a new film we really want to see, we generally watch classic films, or horror films, or if we can find them, really cheesy B movies from the 50s.

"How about a classic horror film?"

I smiled. "Or maybe *The Giant Claw* again?" I said, naming the B movie with the worst effects we'd ever seen. He smiled with only the corners of his mouth and put his credit card in the air to signal to the waitress we were done.

Forensics, Forensics, Where Are You When I Need You

"**Y**ou've reached Daisy."

"Hi, Daisy," I said, so glad she'd picked up and hadn't given me a phone number that was never answered and just went to an endless set of AI telephone routing choices and voicemail boxes guaranteed to lose any communication you wanted to actually deliver or get a response to. "This is Sophie Drake, the PI from the cigarette store fire."

"Nice to hear from you," said Daisy, and it sounded like she actually meant it.

"I was hoping you could give me some more information on the body."

"Let's have coffee," she said. "Say six?"

"Sure. Text me where."

"Will do. Thanks for calling." I got the idea from her breezy voice that she was in her office and didn't want anyone to know she was talking to a PI. Which was fine, because it also probably meant that she was planning to tell me things that would actually be helpful and not just hold back.

"Bye," I said.

"Bye, bye," she responded like a small child.

I looked down as my phone beeped almost immediately. "CAFE DULCE, LITTLE TOKYO, 6 p.m."

I was moderately surprised. I thought all coffee meetings were held in Starbucks these days, but I knew Cafe Dulce. It was in the Japanese Village, the kind of place where you could get a matcha latte and a steamed bun and wander the tourist-trap stores of the artificial heart of Little Tokyo. The only good news was that driving into Downtown at that time of the day was slightly less painful than driving out of it. Not much less painful but slightly.

I was sitting on one of the few seats outside with a latte in hand when Daisy walked up. She ran up to me like a friend. "Oh, so glad you are here," she said as if she was afraid she was going to be stood up. "I need to get a drink, then let's talk."

I watched her bounce over to the counter and order her drink. I wondered how old she was. How young you had to be to still have that kind of springiness, that kind of excitement. She worked in the medical examiner's office. Shouldn't she be depressed by nature? Shouldn't working with corpses make you at least a little glum?

And if that hadn't sucked all the joy out of her, she also worked with cops. I mean, hell. I used to be a cop. They are not the world's happiest people. I watched her flirt with the guy behind the counter as she picked out a pastry. She was young, under thirty. It was the only explanation. She still thought everything in life was possible.

I envied her.

She came down with a large green matcha drink and a healthy-looking muffin. "I hope you don't mind," she said. "I am hungry."

"Go for it. What can you tell me about the body?"

"Well, it's a woman. Early twenties."

"Did she die in the fire?"

"Nope, she died before the fire. Someone hit her from behind. Her skull was caved in."

"You're sure?"

"Yes, we're sure. She died before the fire. We aren't sure exactly how long before the fire." Daisy took a big bite of her muffin, then covered her mouth with her hand so I couldn't see her eating.

"What I can tell you is that it was a while at least, because she was pretty much completely decomposed before she burned. At least that's what the burn patterns look like. Also, the fire burned very, very hot, so the bone is almost like ceramic. The only thing that's not making sense is that the bones seem to be lacking in calcium. Like she had osteoporosis, but she was a young woman, so that doesn't make sense."

"Osteoporosis?"

"Yeah. The bones just aren't calcified as much as we would expect. My boss thinks that it might be how long the bones were in the building, but I think that the girl was sick. I mean, it's pretty obvious she's in her mid-20s from the clavicle fusing."

"Ok, explain this to me like I have no idea what you are talking about, because I have no idea what you are talking about."

"Ok. We are born with three hundred bones but as we get older they fuse together. One of the last ones to start fusing is the clavicle. It starts at about 25. This girl's clavicle had started to fuse, but it's not completely fused, which you would expect it to be by the time she was about thirty. The thing is that twenty-five or thirty is also when her bone mass should have been the highest, but her bone mass is more like that of an old woman. We call it osteopenia. Her bone mass density is far lower than it should be."

"Why?"

"Well, she might have been starved as a child but probably not, because she was 5'7", which is a very average height. So we think she might have been ill."

"Ill?"

"Several diseases can reduce your bone mass, including diabetes and thyroid issues, as well as some viruses like HIV. We are going to try to get some DNA and hope that gives us more information, but right now our best guess is that she was about 24-26 years old at the time of her death and she died and decomposed before the fire began."

"So when do you think she died?"

"See, that's the thing. A body can be turned into bones in a couple of weeks, or it could be as long as 20-plus years."

Ukulele Orchestra is an Oxymoron

I go to family get-togethers with the level of nervous anxiety and stress that's usually only seen in soldiers with PTSD going back to the front.

I arrived at the time I had been ordered to do so. It was, of course, an hour early because she had given me the wrong time. I turned off the Offspring song I'd been screaming along with as I pulled through the parking lot. She was ready to go when I arrived. Standing outside the door, a ukulele in a cardboard box that it had obviously come from the store in.

"Hi, honey," she said as I drove up opening the window. "We need to get over to the hall so I can rehearse a little before the show."

She was all a dither. Hair perfect, makeup perfect, she was wearing that dress I'd given her two Christmases ago that she was saving for best. I'd never seen it on her before. It looked nice. She opened the door of the car and looked in on me in my jeans and a Green Day t-shirt.

"Oh." She sighed. "I should have told you to dress better. Should we go find something in my closet for you?"

"No, Moms." I smiled. "You are in a hurry, and I'm not going to be the one on stage. You are."

"Oh, yes, of course. Do I look ok?"

"You look lovely, Mom. I haven't seen you in that dress before. It is a great color on you."

"Your dad would have loved this dress," she said, and now I felt sorry for her. That seemed to be how it went. I was either annoyed at her or sorry for her. I wanted to just love her but I wasn't sure how to do that. It just wasn't easy.

The instructor for the class, the conductor for the orchestra, came in before the show and my mom introduced him to me energetically. He was a good-looking man. She wasn't wrong about that. He was, however, about fifty. A little too old for me and a little too young for her, which was possibly the worst age group ever, because Mother thought he was hot. And she thought I should think he was hot. If he'd been ten years older, she wouldn't have been trying to introduce him to me at all. She would have just been dating him. And it was obvious that he liked her too.

"Oh, Mrs. Drake, you're here. So good to see."

"Oh, you know, my name's Linda. Call me Linda."

Yes. It's strange. Sometimes I realize that my mother has a first name. Most of the time I just think of her as Mom. And the idea that her name is actually Linda fails me completely. I have to struggle for it. Linda Drake, my mother, queen of all, retired nurse, widow and friend. Everybody likes Linda. Everybody thinks she is great. My friends, when I was younger, thought that she was immense fun. Because she was the cool mom that would take us to see the R-rated movies because she herself wanted to see the latest vampire filk.

Still not sure why she thought it was ok to take me and all my friends to *Resident Evil* for my tenth birthday, but it was memorable. My mother had a way to humiliate and embarrass me when I was younger and I think I've grown out of it. I think I'm finally old enough that she doesn't have any power over me—and then here we are. "Sophie, say hello to Brian. He's a great instructor, you know." She put her hand on his shoulder. "I would never have believed that I could learn so much so quickly. You know, Sophie, when you were younger you were very musical."

"No I wasn't."

"Oh, she doesn't remember. She was, you know. She took after my mother. She could have been a great pianist but she never practiced."

"Nice to meet you, Sophie."

"Hi, Brian."

"You know, I'm sure Brian could give you lessons. We could get you a ukulele. I have an extra one. You could come to lessons next week, or maybe you could give private lessons."

"I have time on Tuesdays for private lessons."

"Well, that settles it then, Sophie. Next Tuesday—"

"Perhaps you would like a private lesson yourself, Mom?" I asked, mortified and wishing I'd never come to visit her at all.

"You aren't working right now—"

"Yes, I am, Mom."

"Oh, your mom said you were between jobs," said Brian.

"Yes, I was, but right now I'm investigating a series of arsons and possible murder.

"Brian stared at me, looking a little confused. I felt the need to explain. From what my mother had said to him he thought I was some kind of unemployed layabout. My mom had worked as a nurse until my parents both retired. I know she worked hard, but she had always considered that I didn't really work. When I was a police officer she had at least understood what I did. I may not have kept the house clean enough or worked hard enough for her, but now that I was a PI and my work came and went she understood even less what I did or why I wasn't available for her every whim.

"I'm a private investigator," I said to Brian."You're not what I would picture for a PI," he said.I smiled. Brian really was a nice guy. Not what I would picture for a ukulele orchestra conductor, but then I wasn't actually sure that I'd ever imagined "ukulele orchestra conductor" as someone's job description. The other old ladies were coming into the social hall.

My mother turned and saw a friend—"Oh hello, Sally."—and I took this opportunity to leave Brian and her and go sit down in the back of the hall waiting for the concert to start.

In all fairness the music was probably better than some of the concerts my mother sat through when I was at school. The pieces they picked to play were not easy, and some of the women played quite well. My mother was not one of those women. Her timing was off and I couldn't work out whether it was because her fingers were swollen and clumsy from years of abuse or whether it was because she was going deaf. Although she'd worked for, or maybe because she'd worked in, a hospital all her life, it was very hard for me to get her to visit a doctor, but perhaps I needed to get her to a doctor and get her ears checked.

While the bunch of ukuleles screeched through a version of *My Country, 'Tis of Thee* I was thinking about my arsonist. Or was I thinking about a murderer? Were the earlier arsons supposed to cover up killings? What was wrong with me that I was already assuming there would be other bodies?

I needed to be solving this crime, not listening to out-of-tune ukuleles murder patriotic songs. What did I really know? I knew that the fires were started by someone who had access to airplane fuel. I knew that the person who burned these buildings personally hated Mrs. Arkbari. They were threatening her. This was not an accident. They wanted to hurt her.

So that ruled out Mike Way and his men. It ruled out Speedy Spark Electrical. And only one person had easy access to airplane fuel. At this point he was really the prime suspect. He knew Mrs. Arkbari. But there was no evidence that he hated her.

I knew Mrs. Arkbari was an objectionable woman, but what had she actually done to make someone hate her enough to try to burn her buildings? The arsonist had endangered themselves and other people to try to burn the buildings. So they had to have a good reason to have done it. I didn't know enough about the people involved. Now that the suspects' list was down from a few million to a handful of people working at Bronson Construction, I needed to know more about all of them. I went to pick up my phone and start trolling the social media of Phil. I looked up for a moment and saw my mother giving me the evil eye. I'd felt it subconsciously even before I looked up, so I put the phone down again.

More than the question of motive, there was also the question of means.

How hard was it really to buy airplane fuel? I guess that was going to be the next thing—going to have to try to buy some plane fuel. I wondered how I'd go about that. Just walk up to an airport and say, "Hey, can I get a little jet fuel for my lawnmower?"

The song was over. I and the five poor husbands who had been tortured both with the ukulele rehearsal in their homes for weeks as well as this concert of the tortured strings all clapped as required.

Another song started and it took me a while to realize it was *When the Saints Go Marching In*. Much like the case I was working on, all the notes were there. All the evidence was there if I could see it. The notes were just all over the place, and not where I thought they should be. They weren't forming the pattern I was expecting. This case felt the same way. The body had been a surprise. It didn't feel like part of the same tune. It felt like someone in the orchestra was playing *Silent Night* while everyone else was playing *When the Saints*. I listened. Yep, someone was playing *Silent Night*. I looked at my mom. She wasn't really playing anything, just strumming along without trying to hit any notes. I looked over at Brian. He had a look of pain on his face. If I were the arsonist and someone started playing a different tune by planting a dead body in my building, I think it would give me pain.

I needed to look for someone who was in pain. Disturbed by the arrival of a body. If the body wasn't part of their plan, if this wasn't some strange jazz tune they were playing, then they weren't expecting the body to show up. This was going to throw them off their game. It might even stop them burning the next building, but it also might make them lash out at Mrs. Arkbari.

The clapping was starting again and I joined in. Then the music, or at least the noise, stopped. Apparently the entire concert was really only about four songs. I couldn't have been happier. I stayed sitting in my seat and waited for my mom to come to me as soon as she stopped congratulating the rest of the orchestra.

"So, Sophie, what did you think?" She came smiling up to me.

"I think it was quite amazing. You must have worked very hard to learn all those songs."

"Oh yes." She beamed. "I mean, I forgot a few notes, but that's to be expected, and it was pretty hard to keep up. But I'm getting better all the time."

"I think you did great, Mom." And I did. I had to admire her. I hoped if I was ever left as a widow I wouldn't be afraid to learn new things and make a complete ass of myself in front of my child. Actually, I just hoped I'd get to the point in my life where I'd be a wife and have a child. Phil might actually make a good dad, I thought, if he wasn't actually a murderer or a serial arsonist.

I was wondering what Phil would look like naked as I followed my mom to the back of the hall where someone had set up a table filled with cupcakes and macaroni salad, hot dogs and bread buns. And for the next two hours I tried to focus on just being with my mom and avoiding her barbs so I could say I had done my duty and would be free for another couple of weeks.

When I went to hug her and kiss her goodbye, she said, "Thank you for coming out. I love you."

"I love you too, Mom," and it is true, even if sometimes she freezes my heart and breaks it in her hands.

Facebook is Less Fun When it Isn't Cat Videos

As soon as I woke up Sunday morning I'd fired up my laptop and lay on my bed. I had the notes from the case on the empty pillow next to me, and my legs crossed to hold the screen up, and I started to research all of the employees of Bronson Construction.

Ok, I admit it, I started with Phil. I wanted to know if he was secretly against *Roe v. Wade*, or anything truly unforgivable, or just possibly a murderer and arsonist. I realized as I started to look through his social media that he was at least forty. Almost nothing in his Instagram, and his Facebook had friends inviting him to his twenty-year high school reunion two years ago. Ok, not friends, perhaps, but people he'd been to school with that because of Facebook decided that he must obviously want to talk to them now, whether or not they had ever had a conversation in high school. He had commented back to all of them very politely. He'd posted about his father's funeral, and was tagged in some photos as Uncle Phil in some of his sister's family shots. He had two sisters, one brother, and grew up in Ohio. Now, I know the new generation uses Ohio as a derogatory word, but even before that I always had a kind of a funny feeling when I heard someone was from Ohio. As if they were going to be so much purer than me, or too foreign, or something. Especially if they said they were from a town like Cincinnati, Ohio, because that just seemed like an odd place to be from. Like coming from the dark side of the moon. My one visit to Ohio (Lima, Ohio, to be exact) had not dispelled the idea that Ohio and California were perhaps the two far spectrums of a place ironically called the *United* States.

And that was almost all he had there. There was more on his LinkedIn profile. All the jobs he'd ever held. He'd worked everywhere for a long time. He'd left his last job when the company went bankrupt. He was loyal. He'd gone to Ohio State for college. All that was missing was why he'd ended up in California. I decided to troll his friends to find out the answer.

Her name was Susie Friend, and she still commented on his posts and liked all his photos. She was also now married to a man called Marvin Friend, and she was still trying to make it in Hollywood as an actress. Susie's MySpace page was still out on the web with photos of Phil and her when they'd first moved to Los Angeles together and moved into a studio apartment in Van Nuys. It was a true shithole. I pulled out his credit report, and took a look at the houses he owned now. He owned some really nice places.

I could see no real reason to keep investigating Phil except that he had admitted that he had access to airplane fuel. In fact, his profile shot was him in a small aircraft above Los Angeles, and it looked absolutely terrifying, like being in a sardine can suspended over the world, ready to fall to your death. My stomach turned at the thought of the claustrophobia and heights.

There were no red flags on social media about him. Maybe in the future that in itself will be a red flag, but for now I needed to go check everyone else in his company.

Amanda's social media was much like herself, cold and impersonal, with photos of places she'd been and things she'd seen. Apparently all the places she'd visited were devoid of humans and animals. It was like looking at the Facebook version of postcards—nice sunsets and no soul. No red flags as such either. Her 42 friends were all women whom she'd known since college. I did go back far enough just for fun to see her ex-husband and honestly, she was better off alone.

I figured I'd probably better check out Francisco, the owner of Bronson Construction. He'd probably dealt with Mrs. Arkbari more than anyone, and although I couldn't see why it would be in his best interests to be burning buildings of your number one client who pretty much paid all your bills, humans have been known to do things that are definitely not totally logical. Case in point, my Tinder date now, two weeks ago. Well, social media-wise Francisco was a blank slate, all promotions for his company and a couple of pictures his wife had posted of his three girls playing soccer with their dad. The people he really seemed to know from his large list of "friends" were few. Only a few people commented on his posts, and most of them seemed to be related in some way or subcontractors he'd used. I checked his credit report as well, and it seemed like he was doing ok—large lines of credit which were all being paid down each month and no real debt.

Then there were the guys underneath Phil. I started with Armando, who as expected had no real social media presence. He also had no real credit either. He'd worked his whole life in construction jobs in an industry where even those people who were not illegal aliens needed Spanish to speak to their coworkers, and it didn't matter that Armando had been born in East Los Angeles and was a US citizen. He'd been a wetback all his life. Actually a sweat back. He'd worked his ass off. I found one of his daughters on Instagram and she was showing off the house Dad had built for her and her kid on the back of his property. His other daughter was at UCLA. Of all the people I'd met, my gut had told me it wasn't Armando, and I couldn't see any reason to change my mind.

Sometimes in the late night I realize how unlucky I am, that I've never really caught the kind of luck that other people take for granted. The kind of luck that gives you a steady relationship, family and friends, a stable job, a stable life, a house paid off before you die. And people who miss you at your funeral. In some ways Armando was a very lucky man.

I picked Rob as my next stalking victim. His Instagram was full of pictures he'd taken. His first selfie at three, and he hadn't stopped since. If he stopped posting, his mother would probably know he was dead before the authorities notified her. Between all the noise it was hard to see who Rob was. What did he think or feel? Did he hate anyone? Let alone Mrs. A? Did he feel anything at all? Were there any thoughts going through his head? He never reposted anything, not even a joke or a meme. I don't know if he thought anything was funny. But there was a photo of almost every time he'd ever taken his shirt off, and another five hundred photos of him drinking every kind of alcohol ever made, and so many photos of bongs and joints that he was just lucky he was living in a state where that was legal. His Instagram never mentioned any kind of work, except that he was an influencer, and that he was helping his friend Carine's Only Fans page. I had less than no desire to check out Carine's Only Fans page. In fact his Instagram page was making me feel old, dirty, and an obnoxious holier-than-thou bitch. I wanted to just sit him down and give him a lecture about what was appropriate and what wasn't.

I also wanted to track down his mom and tell her that she needed to take her boy in hand.

So it was definitely time to walk away. And also damn late. Trolling the net even for work was such a massive time suck. I was sure Harry wouldn't want me to turn in a timesheet that said "Spent ten hours looking at Instagram and two hours watching porn on Only Fans, but don't worry, Rob is innocent." I was pretty sure Rob was not my guy either.

That left Steve, Freddie, Mario and Peet, and me needing to sleep before the sun came up.

I was hoping that while I slept everything would just make sense. That somehow my unconscious brain would know more than my conscious. It was only two days since the last fire. So if the pattern continued we had five days till the next fire. If I didn't find the arsonist by then, there could be more dead bodies. Either they were killing people and putting them in the fires, or the fire itself could kill people. Whoever was doing this didn't care whom they hurt. Five more days to find the answer or another building went up and in it possibly another woman.

These are the happy fairytales I tell myself before I sleep. Because if sleep is not coming easily enough, then telling myself that I may cause the death of some innocent woman by not getting my job done quickly enough is definitely going to act as a lullaby.

I stared at the ceiling for too long before I fell asleep without finding any kind of solution.

And the Threats Keep Rolling In

I was woken by the angry buzzing of a phone on mute. I lay there for a moment wondering why I was awake then heard it again—a text message, and another text message and then as I tried to peel my eyes open, another.

I tried rolling over again and going back to sleep. It was probably just my mother with some emergency, like the last time she'd woken me early because her friend Mary needed to visit a dentist and did I know a dentist in Mexico that was cheap? Since if my mother ever paid attention when I spoke she would know that I have never actually been to a dentist in Mexico, I obviously know five or six of them.

It buzzed again. I picked the phone up. It was 8:15 a.m. That wasn't too early, not when you'd fallen asleep at about four. I looked at the messages bleary-eyed. They weren't from my mom. I sat up and rubbed my eyes, trying to focus.

They were from Maria.

Oh crap.

I read them at once like one long letter.

"There is a new threatening letter. I called the police already. Spoke to Detective Longe—he's been assigned the case. Please come. He wants to kill her," said Maria in the texts. Even by text she was polite and used punctuation. There should be brownie points to get into heaven if you use punctuation.

I texted back. "On my way."

Then called Harry.

"Are you there yet?" said Harry when I called in.

"On my way, your friend Detective Longe I on his way too.

"I didn't think you were going. I will meet you there."

He hung up. I had apparently also missed eight calls from Harry. No voicemails, of course. Harry knew me better than that. I threw my clothes on and started to drive. Then I realized I didn't actually know where I was going.

I wasn't going to call Harry; he was already disappointed enough in me. So I asked Siri to call Maria.

"Hi, Maria."

"Oh, Sophie, it's horrible. What he said. Oh my. Mrs. Arkbari is mad at me for calling the police."

"We will talk to the police, Maria. It's ok. Harry and I are both coming to you. Now, where was the letter delivered? The office? Or the house?"

"The office, with this morning's mail."

"Ok. Where is Mrs. Arkbari right now?"

"She's on her way to the office too."

I pushed in the address of their office into my GPS. "I'll be there in twenty-five minutes, Maria. I assume you want us to meet you at your office."

Better make sure before I drove twenty-five minutes in the wrong direction. The police would probably, but not necessarily, arrive before me. This wasn't really a police emergency, and I kind of hoped that the police were busy with a real emergency so that Harry or I was there to talk to them when they arrived. Maria was definitely too excited to talk to them, and Mrs. A might just tell them to go away, which was also not helpful.

"I assume you spoke to Detective Longe?" I said, hoping I'd remembered the name right since I couldn't look at my notebook.

"Oh yes, and he said he'd be here in about an hour."

"Great. Send me his contact card and I'll give him a call while I'm on my way in," I said. "Hang tight, Maria. It's going to be ok."

She hung up and I dialed Detective Longe.

"Longe," he answered as if his name alone was enough to answer any question.

"Hi. I'm Sophie Drake. I'm calling about the threats against Mrs. Arkbari. I'm a private eye that was hired by her."

"Yes. I hear there's been another one. I am on my way to the office."

"I am as well. Mrs. Arkbari would like to stay out of this as much as possible and has asked if I can speak with you. I'm on my way to her office now, and I was hoping to meet with you there."

"Sure," said Detective Longe. "But I will need to speak with Mrs. Arkbari."

"She won't be at the office," I looked down at the time on my GPS growing, "for at least another forty-five minutes, so if you could be at the office after that she would be available."

"Ok, I'll arrive sometime after nine thirty," said Longe, probably calculating that if he didn't have to leave till nine he'd avoid some traffic. In Los Angeles people do the craziest things to avoid traffic, even getting up for work at five a.m. and arriving an hour early so their commute is only an hour, not two.

"Did you get any fingerprints off the last threat letter?" I asked casually, because Harry had probably already followed up on this. I'd just forgotten to ask.

"No, nothing."

"Ok, so we probably won't find any on this one either. Good to know. See you there. Thanks."

Longe hung up and I hoped I hadn't pissed him off at all. I hadn't been having the best of luck not pissing off authorities this week. Between Jeff Delmonico the arson investigator and Detective Fuck-off at the cigarette factory fire, I was beginning to wonder if I'd completely lost my touch.

I arrived to see Harry standing outside with Mrs. Arkbari. She was sitting on her walker and he was bent down, talking to her. I felt like a kid who'd arrived late to a parent-teacher meeting and knew the grownups had been talking about them behind their back.

Taking a deep breath, I walked up to them. Mrs. Arkbari looked muted, smaller, almost frail, like she had been crying. Harry looked up at me. "Let's go back inside." He opened the door and she shuffled in on her walker. I followed them into the office. The threat letter was lying on the desk where it had been opened and no one was going near it. Maria was standing over near the coffee machine, not so much getting coffee as avoiding that letter. I wondered what it said that it could have humbled Mrs. Arkbari.

I walked up to it. The print was big enough to read without getting close.

YOU ARE A MURDERER!
I WILL MAKE YOU PAY!

I didn't know what Harry had already asked, and because I have no natural-born tact I asked the first question that came into my mouth. I would say that came into my mind but if I had, in fact, thought about it for ten seconds before I said something I probably would have said nothing.

"So is that the first serious threat?"

"No," said Mrs. Arkbari, and everyone turned to her because apparently no one else had thought to ask that question, or maybe everyone else had been too polite. She turned to Harry to justify her answer. "You see, I just didn't think they were being serious before. The first few letters they told me to come clean and admit my crime, and I just thought it was a joke. Well, not funny, but not serious. They said I would pay for my crimes. I don't understand why they think I'm a murderer."

"Could be the murdered girl in the building?" I said before Harry's evil eye could shut me down.

"I'm not responsible for that. How could anyone think I could be responsible for murdering someone?"

The phone rang and Maria went to take the call while carefully not getting too close to the threatening letter.

"Hello. You've reached ABF. Maria speaking. Yes. Oh. All right, thank you for calling. Yes, I will let her know. Goodbye." Maria looked up from the phone, her face paler.

Maria put down the phone and turned to her boss. "Mrs. Arkbari, someone just lit the warehouse building on 4th Street."

Mrs. Arkbari bit her lip and shook her head. "That was one of my father's last purchases before he died."

I had to respect that a woman her age could still remember details like that. I had a hard time remembering what my last address was, let alone when in time anything happened. When did my dad die? Was it before I moved, I became a cop, or after? I tried to remember now if I'd seen him at the sheriff department graduation. All I could remember was sitting at the graduation trying so hard to not go to sleep, because I'd gone out the night before on a celebratory bender and been barely functional that day. Yes, I think he was there. I think he was probably proud of me before he died. I hope he was.

It was funny to me that this woman had a sentimental attachment to a building. My dad had never left me anything. The few things he owned were still my mom's things—her car, her furniture, her boxes of junk piled high for the day I would need to go through it all. When that day came I would probably be happy if it all burned.

"That warehouse has a fire suppression system," said Mrs. Arkbari. And I admired how much this woman retained and knew. At her age you would think she would be losing some of her memory or sanity but she seemed quite a bit more lucid than me, and definitely more than my mother. "Won't that stop it from burning?" she said, looking at Harry.

"Interesting. Yes, one would hope so," he said, and he picked up his phone.

"Hi. Mr. Jeff Delmonico, Arson Investigator, please." Harry had the kind of voice that didn't encourage questions and he was put straight through. Harry put his phone on speaker.

"Jeff Delmonico speaking. How may I help you?"

"This is Harry Nelson. We have been speaking about the arsons in Hollywood and Los Angeles, the ones that were started with airplane fuel."

"Yes," said Jeff, his voice dropping to a level that indicated dread, and a little contempt. "How can I help you, Harry?"

"There's a new fire, just started. The building is also owned by my client, Mrs. Arkbari. It's on 4th Street and..." Harry looked up at Maria for an answer.

"4th and Seaton, in the Arts District," answered Maria.

"Did you hear that? 4th and Seaton. Arts District. Same neighborhood as the last fire. But this time the property has a fire suppression system."

"That will help..." said Jeff, "burn less of the evidence. Thank you for letting me know. I will go there now and see what the state of the situation is."

"Great," said Harry. "How long do you think it will take for you to enter the property if the fire suppression system worked?"

"Depends on the type of system, but probably an hour or so."

"Ok, great. We'll meet you down there in a couple of hours." Harry hung up and turned to Maria. "Thanks, doll. I wonder if there is any way we can see if the place burned to the ground."

"KQLA news online," said Maria. "They are always too bored so they show every little car chase, house fire, and freeway pileup. I am sure they will have a 'copter looking at a warehouse fire downtown just in case it turns into a good story."

Maria went to her computer, still standing, leaning over the letter as if it was poison where it lay next to her keyboard. She typed in carefully, then hit some buttons and sent the internet feed she was looking at on her computer to the TV on the wall in front of us.

"This is KQLA with the Sky Eye. We've got smoke near the 4th Street bridge. Police scanners indicate that this is a warehouse fire.""What can you tell us about it, Jim?" said the overly made-up woman in a suit behind the desk back at the studio.

"It's a three-alarm fire. They aren't taking any chances; it's too close to Downtown. They have closed off the 4th Street bridge and most of the traffic downtown is being redirected. I am hoping, Shirley, that this won't be a fire like the one last week in the smoke shop that closed down traffic for hours and made the commute home almost impossible for so many people."

"Yes, Jim, and our sources tell us that they are still investigating the possible causes of last week's fire and also the body that was found within. It seems odd, Jim, to have two fires in less than a week so close to each other. Any ideas?"

"I don't know if they are related or not, Shirley. This fire looks different than last week's one. Last week's one burned for almost five hours before the firemen were able to get it under control. The fire trucks have surrounded the building and they are doing the sur-round and drown method of firefighting. The building is a suspected pot-growing location and getting inside is not going to be easy."

"Jim, we are going to cut to Alicia. She's our eyes on the ground there at the developing situation on 4th Street." The screen went from the aerial shot to the reporter in the street, whose bleach-blonde, care-fully straightened hair was being blown around in the wind created by the fire behind her. "Hi, Alicia. What can you tell us about the building?"

"Well, Shirley, the firemen are telling me that this fire is under control and that they should be able to get it a hundred percent contained very soon. The property was being used to grow marijuana and there was a fire prevention system installed, which has taken all of the recycled irrigation water and fresh water into a supercharged system where it was dispensed as a mist as soon as the heat detectors were triggered. "

"Wow, that's lucky," said Shirley with the voice of despair that the one piece of bad news she thought was going to keep her with some-thing to say all day was quickly getting solved.

"It looks like this one is almost out. One of the fire trucks is leaving the scene and the smoke seems to be dissipating," said Alicia. "The firemen are telling us that the building had two separate systems for fire management, one on the grow area and another with foam in the office section of the building."

Shirley's face was falling even futher.

Alicia banged her earpiece. "I am just getting a report that there has been a body found in the building."

"Really," said Shirley, immediately happier. "What can you tell us about the body? Is this fire connected to the fire earlier in the week where the mysterious body of a woman was found? What do we know so far, Alicia?"

"I am unable to confirm that this fire is related to last week's fire, Shirley. We'll keep you updated as this story develops."

The screen went back to Shirley at the studio, who started to introduce a story about a new scam involving pet owners when Maria cut it off.

I had been watching Mrs. Arkbari while the news was talking. I have this bad habit of watching the people watching the TV, instead of watching the TV. Drove my last boyfriend insane. Said he couldn't watch anything with me because he was the show. Trying to convince him that he was just more interesting and more sexy than the movie star on the screen did not work as well as I thought it should. When the news said that another body had been found in the next building, Mrs. Arkbari did not look shocked, or surprised.

Maria looked shocked and horrified, I could feel the shock in myself, Harry grunted a little, but Mrs. A just looked sad. Not scared, not angry, not surprised. Her mouth just pulled down a little. Not much but a little. She wasn't surprised. Just sad.

Why?

If Jeff Delmonico, Arson Investigator, was right, then of course there would be a body in this building, and bodies may still yet be found at the first two fire sites, because these fires were to cover up murders. But in the last two weeks no one had found an extra body or two lying around in the first two fires. And I didn't think the fires and the bodies were related. The last fire had a murdered girl in it. My idea was that if the arsonist were a killer, then he wouldn't react to a body being found at the scene. But if the arsonist and the killer were not the same person, then the arsonist would be thrown from their game and become erratic because of the unexpected corpse.

The arsonist till now had been slow and calculated. He'd followed a pattern. It hadn't been seven days since the last fire. The first three fires were exactly a week apart. I wasn't expecting another fire until the week was over. This fire and this new threat calling Mrs. Arkbari a murderer were not calculated. The arsonist was angry. Someone was playing *Silent Night* in the middle of their *America the Beautiful*. And the arsonist thought that it was Mrs. Arkbari. That Mrs. Arkbari was a murderer.

I looked at her. It wasn't just that she wasn't capable of committing the crime at this point in her life. After all, we didn't know when the last victim had been killed. It could have been when Mrs. Arkbari was much younger. And it's a hard-core fact that killing someone by coming up behind them and hitting them on the head with something heavy doesn't require that much skill, or strength, or even planning. Just walk up behind someone with something heavy and slam them good. If you have the right tool, and a bit of knowledge, killing some-one is so much easier than it really should be. I was sure she was actually capable of a murder, but that look of sadness, that second where her mouth went down told me she hadn't done it.

She wasn't our murderer. But she knew more than she was telling and getting her to talk was going to be just slightly more difficult than working out who had burned these last four buildings. I really hoped it wasn't Phil. He'd texted me last night and just said hi, and it had been so sweet and nice. I could only hope I wasn't going to be sending him to jail soon.

"Let's go to the building," said Mrs. Arkbari, standing up without aid of her walker, determined and ready to go.

"They won't let us near it yet. We won't get within two blocks," I said, being sensible. She stared at me with the eyes of a woman who has never heard the word no.

"Sophie's right," said Harry, helping her sit back down in her seat.

The door opened. "Hello. I'm looking for the offices of Mrs. Arkbari."

We all looked up, and there was someone who was obviously Detective Longe. No one but a police detective could be wearing a forest-green polyester suit in Los Angeles in August. In a city that doesn't wear suits or ties he looked hot and bothered, as unseemly as a Mormon in a clothing-optional tropical resort. I had forgotten he was coming, and from the look on everyone else's face I wasn't the only one. He was almost all the way through the door before Maria remembered her manners and invited him in.

"Please come on in, Detective. We were expecting you. The letter that I called you about is there," she said, pointing to the desk she had abandoned earlier in the day.

He walked over to it and looked down. Then nodded his head and turned around. "So who's all you people?"

"I am Mrs. Arkbari," she said regally. If she'd had more strength I think she would have stood and put her hand out to be kissed so that he could properly pay respects to her royalty.

"I'm Maria. I'm Mrs. Arkbari's assistant, and I called you, and this is Harry Nelson and Sophie Drake. They are private investigators and have been investigating the arsons since the second fire," Maria said like she was the court announcer and it was her job to make sure everyone who came to the ball was properly announced. Detective Longe looked Harry up and down and grunted slightly in approval. His eyes passed over me like I was wallpaper and went back to Mrs. Arkbari.

"So how many threats have you had?"

"About ten, I think," she said.

"But you didn't contact our office before this?"

"No. Well, I didn't think it was anything important, you know. I thought someone was just blowing off some steam and would go away."

"Were all the letters like this?"

"Oh no," Mrs. Arkbari said, raising herself to her full height in the chair. "The first few were just vague. They said I was going to pay. This is the first one that said that I was a murderer."

"Pay for what?"

"I don't know. I wasn't worried because there is nothing I've ever done that's been a reason to be angry at me. Not like this."

Mrs. Arkbari was answering better for a man than she had for me. I watched her face. There was something. She was thinking about something, something she wasn't saying. What she was saying was the truth but behind that was the little sad face when the next body was found in the next building. Behind the truth was something else, something bigger, something she hadn't told us, the police, or anyone.

"There has been another fire in one of her downtown buildings in Los Angeles this afternoon. The TV said they found another body. But we don't know if it's true."

He sighed. "What was the address?"

Maria told him and he walked outside to make a private call.

We watched him through the windows pacing back and forth. And we said nothing because there was nothing left to say and no one who wanted to hear.

The News Never Gets the Story Right

Detective Longe walked back in shaking his head. "The news was wrong."

"See? Nothing to worry about, ma'am. There was no dead body," said Maria.

"The news is often wrong," said Harry.

"The news report said there was one dead body found in the building," said Longe, "but there are three."

THREE! I screamed to myself. *THREE!* How the hell do you find three bodies in a fire? Were three people killed in the fire? How does this happen? Didn't the fire suppression system get everyone out before the fire went up? The fire didn't even burn the whole building. How could three people die?

"The skeletons of no less than three women have been found in the wall where the fire started."

"They didn't die in the fire?" I said, a little relieved that my failure to solve the case hadn't just killed three people.

"The remains have been there some time. Forensics are examining the corpses and we will be cordoning off the building until further investigations are done."

"What do you mean, further investigations?" asked Mrs. Arkbari.

"We have reason to believe there may be more bodies in the building and we will be looking for them. I will need a statement from you. When did you purchase the building?" He sat down and pulled out a notebook. This was a real interrogation now. "How long have you owned the building?"

"I don't know. Give your questions to Maria, Detective, and my lawyer will give you any answers you need."

"You want me to speak to your lawyer?"

"Yes. Send your questions to Maria and then my lawyer will review them and be in touch," said Mrs. Arkbari.

Mrs. A was lying. She remembered exactly when that building was purchased. And everything about it, including the tenants and the fire suppression system. If she was lying about this, what else was she lying about? Did she pay someone to burn her buildings? Was she in some kind of financial trouble and needed the buildings burned for insurance? Was she a killer who was even now, at the end of her life, trying to hide her crimes?

The detective got up to leave, recognizing a brick wall when he saw one. Maria gave him a card and he picked up the threat letter to take for analysis.

I looked at Harry and Harry looked at me. His face was a mirror of mine. What the fuck kind of shit were we really dealing with?

Harry and I sat across from each other at Tallyrand. We'd each driven there in our own cars knowing we needed a few minutes to consult and we may as well do it with a full belly. Debbie walked us to our seats. "You guys want your usual?" she asked.

"Yes, plus a chocolate cream pie and a chocolate shake for me," I said.

"Ok, so it's 'the day sucks' meal. Coming right up," she said and didn't bother giving us menus or anything but just went off to put our order in.

One of the joys of having a regular joint is that they know your order, they know your name, they know you. Of course, this is also one of the worst things about it too.

Debbie showed up with water for each of us, and a kid's coloring set. "In case you need to draw anything out."

I smiled at her as she left it and then left us alone.

"So, kid, tell me what you're thinking first," grunted Harry.

"Mrs. A is lying to us. I don't know what she's not telling us but it's something big. She knows something about these bodies. I don't think she killed anyone but someone did, and I think she knows who."

Harry nodded and started to scratch his shaven gray scalp. I wasn't sure he wasn't actually ripping a skin cancer off, the way he was digging at himself. "And the arsonist?"

"Not sure. Except that the arsonist isn't the killer. I am sure the arsonist isn't the killer. Well, mostly sure. I mean, she could have hired the arsonist. But I don't think so. I think the threat letter today had her genuinely shook. She was all a bother, then there's three more bodies, and all of a sudden she's cool as an iced latte with vanilla foam and asking for a lawyer. But before that... Before that she was shook. Someone called her a murderer and it shook her."

"Yep, that's my take too," said Harry.

Debbie showed up with Harry's coffee and coker, light ice, and the chocolate shake, whipped cream and a straw and a spoon. I smiled up at her. She'd colored her hair again, darker this time to cover the gray. It didn't really suit her as well but she'd made an effort. Effort should be rewarded. "I like your hair, Debbie. It looks really nice." "Thanks, Sophie," she said, fluffing the locks with her hand. "I wanted to try something different. I don't know if I like it or not but in a few weeks it will grow out and I'll probably do something different next time again."

"You are a beautiful woman, Debbie," I said, and it was true, for her beauty was an innate part of her soul, not her hair, or her skin, or her left shoulder, or her freckled knees.

"Do go on," giggled Debbie and walked away.

"So we agree," Harry started to doodle with the crayons on the back of the coloring paper, "that the arsonist is the one who sent the threat letters?"

"Has to be," I said. "No one else has any reason. And the threats have come to pass so, yeah, arsonist is threat-letter boy."

"Boy?"

"Harry, do I have to tell you what the statistics on women committing violent crime are? Besides which, the majority of potential suspects are male. And I don't think Maria or Mrs. A torched the places."

"Fair."

"So the arsonist knows that someone is a murderer. Arsonist thinks it's Mrs. Arkbari."

"But you don't think it is," said Harry.

"Nope."

"So who is it?" Harry answered, and I thought about that while I sucked down my milkshake and ate a chicken tostada salad.

I Try to Buy Myself Some Leaded Gasoline

I was still lacking information. I put a text into Daisy and decided it was time to track down the one thing I knew for sure about the arsonist. They had access to airplane fuel. I decided to visit the local little airport in Santa Monica to ask there. Circ told me I could talk to Rudi. He was the guy who ran the airplane rental place Circ sometimes used. I still couldn't work out the best way to thank Circ for getting me the private jet to Vegas for my last case, but I was sure that he'd work out some way to make me pay him back.

I drove into the little parking lot in front of the airport and, as per instructions, texted Rudi. He came out and found me in the parking lot. He was a distinguished-looking man, kind of like Ricardo Montalban at thirty. I cursed my silly vow. It seemed like fate was determined to make me regret all my decisions, even that one.

"Sophie Drake?" he said, walking towards me in a polo shirt, jeans and loafers, so LA-style business wear.

"Yes. Hi."

"Circus called and asked if I could help you. So obviously, anything I can do for you..."

He was leading me back to his office and I followed, happy to get out of the sun. It wasn't the hottest day of the year, and Santa Monica is always a little more temperate, but the gray morning fog had completely burned off and the sun was a little brighter than someone accustomed to indoor lighting and air conditioning is comfortable in.

We walked into his small but well-appointed office and he offered me coffee, and who was I to say no? So I settled myself into a comfortable chair and he made two lattes from a machine that from the moment I saw it was the new first thing on my Christmas wish list, brought them over to the coffee table and sat in a high-back chair across from me.

"So what can I do for you?"

"I am investigating a case involving arson." I pulled up my notes to make sure I got it right. "The accelerant being used is 100LL, which I am told is used to fuel small aircraft."

"Yes, it's 100 octane and low lead."

"I thought leaded gasoline was illegal."

"It is for cars. The fuel planes used to use had more lead—that's why this is the LL, low-lead model."

"So where could I buy it?"

"Airports sell it but it's strictly controlled. We have a fuel farm on-site. You buy the fuel and the fuel farm will fill your tank."

"Fuel farm? You powering your planes with cow dung?"

He smiled. "No, that's just what they call it. Come, I'll show you."

I sucked down the rest of the coffee and followed him out of the office to his golf cart. There's something about seeing an attractive man behind the wheel that changes golf cart from something that old people use because they can't walk around a golf course to one of the best all-terrain sports vehicles ever. And it was with the wind in my face that we drove out onto the runway. I noted that he had to go through two security gates to even get out into the business end of the airport. And when I looked around I could see why. In addition to tiny little aircraft that looked like 1960s *Popular Mechanics* covers, there were larger planes, sleek and beautiful, the modern version of the 1960s dream, yet not the flying cars we'd been promised by the Jetsons.

These were all toys of rich men. Even the little old ones were not things owned or operated by the majority, and here they all were parked, waiting, covering the edges of the runway like so much traffic congestion. Rudi drove us through the parking area and around the runway to the end. There was what looked like a gas station pump system with large tanks next to it and a small fuel truck.

"Most of the little planes are self-service here at Santa Monica," he said. They prepay and then can bring their planes over to fuel. The larger planes, the fuel truck goes to them."

"AV UL94," I read off the side of the pump setup. "What's that?"

"It's 94 octane, unleaded aviation fuel."

"So not the 100LL?"

"No, Santa Monica converted to unleaded, but it's the only airport that's done it so far. Some planes still need the 100LL and Santa Monica still has it. It's just harder to buy. But they are phasing out lead for airplanes just like they did for cars."

"So odds are this wasn't the airport they got the gas from. What other airports are there that have the right gas?"

"The rest of the airports would have it, but the biggest small-plane airport is Whiteman airport in Pacoima. There's Van Nuys as well, but it's bigger, or one of the airports out of the city a bit, like Agua Dulce or Palmdale." I had deliberately deleted off my list all suspects who lived in Agua Dulce or Palmdale because it's too far to drive. But what if the suspect was flying to work? *Stop it,* I yelled at myself. *Stop second-guessing what you've already done. You don't rip a whole puzzle apart just because one piece doesn't fit. You do what your grandma used to do, you shove that piece in no matter what and glue it down before you frame it and stick it on the wall, because in the end no one will notice that one cloud is a little off, so long as the whole picture makes sense.*

As charming as Rudi was, it was time I went and checked out a lower-budget airfield, one whose land wasn't soon going to be covered in million-dollar skyscraper apartments. I was going to start with Pacoima because one should always swallow the frog first and Pacoima was definitely the geographic equivalent of a big, ugly toad.

I drove north into the Valley, the temperature rising steadily. Pacoima is one of those cities that people drive through on their way to somewhere else. The Richie Valens Freeway runs through it, although like most freeways it is only really known by its number, because it's really just a piece of the 5 Freeway. Richie Valens is the only really famous person to ever come from Pacoima or even, I think, stop within its city limits. My only memories of actually going to Pacoima were when my dad was looking for parts for his old Buick and would bring me along to the car junkyards because my little hands could usually reach into places better than his could.

I drove down the streets towards the airport. It was ugly and sad and scary as only a street in a major city in the world's richest country can be. There was a street lined with cars where people lived, and a liquor store that hadn't seen a coat of paint since 1964. And cute little houses, and other little houses where tarpaulins on the roof held down by bricks were the most structural element.

The airport entrance when I approached it looked like a long driveway into a rich person's summer house. The parking lot had a sign for free flights for 8-17-year-olds, and a group of people setting up a picnic in front of some clubhouse-type buildings. I parked in the lot and started to explore.

Everything else was gated off. The runway with tiny little planes, and the rest of the hangars and airport buildings were behind locked gates. I called the number Rudi had given me and Jasmina answered quickly and said she would come get me.

Jasmina turned out to be a beautiful young woman whose attention to detail with the fake eyelashes and long false fingernails, straight hair and perfectly drawn cupid-bow lips were things I could only aspire to. I looked at her and put my hand to my head, trying to remember what grooming I'd done before I left the house. Turned out I'd put my hair up in a scrunchie knot/bun. And I vaguely remembered brushing my teeth. I didn't want to check my armpits because I could tell without careful inspection that I'd either forgotten deodorant this morning or it had failed already.

She'd driven towards me in a golf cart, opening the gate as she came through.

"Hi. You must be Sophie."

"How did you know?"

"Rudi said you were a cute little thing. And you don't look like you are here for the fuel truck driver job."

She motioned for me to sit beside her and we quickly drove to her office.

"You are looking for a fuel truck driver?" I said as we walked in.

"Oh yes, we are always hiring guys for different things around here." She walked behind her desk, grabbed an old-fashioned radio and attached it to her waist. She was about my size. It's always nice to meet a fellow "cute little thing."

"What is your official job title?" "I'm the assistant general manager, which means I do everything. Including HR.

"You must be busy. Thank you so much for speaking with me.""
Rudy thought I should take you for a tour around."

"That would be amazing." I was so happy that Rudi had cleared the
way for me. I hadn't asked him to but he was probably trying to curry
favor from Circus. Circ is so rich he probably doesn't appreciate that
people go out of their way to make his life easier and better. Or maybe
he remembers how the real world works. I must ask him one day. On
the other hand, being a white man in a first-world country, he is already
so overflowing in privilege he's probably immune from seeing it.

I knew that Circ's life had been full of trials but I also knew that in
some ways his life was easier just because he was a man, and he would
never understand how different our trips through the world had been.
I had more in common with this beautiful young woman and her
half-inch fake eyelashes than I had with Circ, despite us growing up
together.

We walked back out to the golf cart and headed out, with her acting
as my tour guide. "We are the largest general aviation airfield in Los
Angeles."

"What's general aviation?"

"Small private planes. We have over 80,000 takeoffs and landings
every year. The airport was started in 1946 as a private general aviation
airport but we are now owned and operated by the County of Los
Angeles."

"How about the fueling? You said something about needing a new
fuel truck driver?" I said as we zipped between parked planes and
around the rather small runway. Of course, when I say rather small
I am comparing it to LAX, which until very recently was the only
airport I'd ever been on the runway of.

"Yes. I'm taking you there now. We have a full service, as well as
self-service fueling."

"Self-serve? So people could just walk up with a can?"

"Oh no, they taxi their planes up to the pump. Although self-service is cheaper, most people still opt for full-service fueling, where the fuel truck comes to their plane and fills the tanks."

"Why wouldn't you save the money and do it yourself?"

"Well, the pumps don't have a shut-off on them. So if you screw up you're doing a lot of cleanup of aviation fuel, and also paying us fines for cleanup. So sometimes it's just easier to pay the trucks. Unless, of course, we don't have a truck available. We just had to fire a driver who worked the night shift, so right now, until I replace him, we don't have twenty-four-hour-a-day service."

"But if I wanted to buy aviation fuel, it would be possible to just walk up to the self-serve pump and fill up a can?"

"It's technically possible. But you'd have to get onto the runway first, which is a little challenging if you don't have a plane or an ID card."

"Do you keep records of everyone who has access?"

She nodded. "Yeah, but then something happens."

"Like what?" I said as she kept driving back around the runway the long way back to her office.

"The county just realized that every time we cleaned the fuel tanks there was a lot of fuel that had to be drained. Anyway, turned out that Joey—he was the fuel truck driver at night—well, anyway, Joey was opening the gates at night and selling all the waste fuel to people."

"Who would want to buy waste fuel?"

"Oh, it's actually good fuel. It's just that our tanks are old so we have to make sure we keep cleaning them often, you know. Anyway, they try to clean them regularly, one tank at a time, and he's supposed to dump the waste but instead he was selling it to street racers."

"Street racers?"

"Yeah, you know, young guys who modify cars and like to race. They like the extra octane of the Avgas. Makes them go faster."

"And anybody could buy that gas?"

"We don't know who Joey sold it to. I heard that the word on the street was that whenever Joey saw on the schedule that a tank cleaning was coming up, he'd put a notice out on a racing message board and a classic car message board. Then people would just line up with gas cans looking for a fill."

"So anyone could have known how to get the gas?"

"Pretty much, and he'd been doing it for years, so all the people who live nearby knew it too. I mean, he was selling the gas cheaper than you buy unleaded at the gas station."

"Wow, so I should have been coming here for a fill-up instead of spending seventy-five dollars yesterday near my house?"

"Probably not. I heard that the lead screws up your catalytic converter eventually. Street racers like to take them off, and of course, classic cars were built for lead so they run better if they have some."

We were back at her office and I was so unexpectedly happy. Phil wasn't the only one with access to the accelerant. It could have been any of them. I needed to ask new questions. And I needed to do it now.

Daisy Loves the Ones Destined to Push Up Daisies

I called Amanda and she told me that all the guys came back from the field about five. They would drop their keys with her and take their own cars home. I had just enough time to get from Pacoima to her office by four.

Driving in LA traffic gives you a lot of time to think. The kind of time where you can either listen to an audiobook or just reconsider all of your life choices. Or in this case, while my car crawled slowly down the 405, I could think about my suspects.

I'd been stuck on the means of doing the crime. And it turned out that it was much easier to get the accelerant than I thought. The nagging question was why? What had Mrs. Arkbari done that was so awful that someone sought revenge? I was sure that Mrs. A was not a murderer, but she hadn't been shocked by the buildings containing dead bodies. At least not as shocked as she should have been.

I needed more information. There were still too many holes in the puzzle, and the pieces that seemed to fit now felt upside down and out of place. I called Daisy at Forensics.

"Hey, Daisy. It's Sophie."

I could hear the smile in her voice. "Give me a second, babe. I'll call you right back."

She hung up, and I knew she was walking out of the office so she could tell me some good stuff. A few seconds later the phone rang. I grabbed it hoping it was her and not my new boyfriend, Potential Spam. I didn't want to talk to Potential Spam despite his potential. It was Daisy.

"Hi, Sophie. So glad you called. Did you hear—it's so exciting—we just got another three bodies from that new fire in the warehouse downtown."

Ok, hearing Daisy so excited about more bodies was unsettling at best. I had to wonder what a good day for her was. Finding a mass grave in a basement? Maybe she should move to one of those countries where finding sites of genocide was like getting the toy out of the bottom of the Lucky Charms cereal, something that formerly you expected and when it was no longer a regular occurrence caused you a little sadness.

"I wondered if you had those already. So what can you tell me about the new bodies? Were they dead before the fire?"

"Oh yes, certainly."

"So if they didn't die in the fire, how did they die?"

"Well, that's what's so cool. They were all women in their early twenties and they all died by being struck on the back of the head. I am guessing they were murdered by the same person who murdered the first woman."

"So the fire was set to cover up the murders?"

"Nope."

"So it was coincidence?"

"My theory," Daisy's voice dropped just a little, "is that the person who set the fire was trying to find more bodies."

"I'm confused."

"The first body we got was all burned up. It was hard to be sure. I mean, I was pretty sure but there would have been some other expert who would have argued I was wrong... But I wasn't. I was right."

"You were right about what?" I said, slamming on my brakes as someone tried to sideswipe me and drive me into the other lane just because they were the king of the road and wanted the lane I was in even if I was in it.

"I thought that Jane Doe #1 had been dead at least 20 years. You know, that she was a cold case. I mean, she had amalgam dental work and no implants and, well, the bones just felt old."

"But you couldn't prove it because..."

"Because the bones were burned at such a high temperature, it just kind of melted them smooth, you know." She sounded like a cheerleader at my high school, except instead of talking about how we were going to beat Burbank High she was babbling excitedly about the remains of some poor murdered woman.

"So the bones were too cooked?"

"Yep, but the remains from today—they hadn't burned at all. I mean, hardly at all. Someone had taken the accelerant and spread it on all the interior walls. So they all started to burn at the same time. And then the fire system stopped the fire. So all the fire did was make holes so we could see the bodies."

"That's what you meant when you said the arsonist was trying to find more bodies?"

"Yep. They knew there were going to be bodies in the walls, and they wanted to make sure people looked at all the walls. And because of the fire suppression system, the bodies weren't all burned up this time. So now we are sure."

"Sure of what?"

"Well, you know I told you that the first body had decalcified bones?"

"Yes. You weren't sure why."

"Well, now I'm sure. The DNA shows HIV virus. It looks like the first corpse had full-blown HIV. That was more common in the past. I think she was a prostitute."

"And do you think these women are too?"

"I think so, and the bodies are in good condition so it will be easier to identify them."

"If they've been there twenty years, why are they in good condition?"

"Oh, I forgot to tell you. It looks like these bodies were mummified in salt before they were put into the walls of the warehouse. We are sure that these are the bodies of people who were killed at least twenty years ago. Maybe even more. The first one was twenty years ago too, so they are connected."

"The fires *are* connected. The warehouse is owned by the same woman as the cigarette shop."

"Oh wow, then I'd be wondering if she was a serial killer."

I sat there for a moment, glad that I could drive on autopilot. Serial killer. There were four bodies, so I guessed Daisy was right. And if Daisy was right maybe these weren't the only bodies. We just hadn't found the rest yet.

"Thanks so much, Daisy," I said, too shook to ask her any more questions. And maybe there were no more questions, or maybe I just didn't know what to ask.

I hung up with Daisy with lots to think about and still more time on the freeway to think. Thinking time is rather limited in this world. Most people don't do any if they can avoid it. There's always the radio or the next streamed show, or viral videos, or anything except time with your head and your thoughts. The fact that people would rather watch the news and see horrible tragedies than sit in the dark with their thoughts for ten minutes pretty much tells you how weak humans have really become. Not that I want to sit and think about my thoughts, my upcoming birthday, my single status, my mother with whom I would soon be celebrating another year of "she's all alone on her daughter's birthday." These are not things I want to think about, but the case? I can think about the case.

Twenty years ago at least four women were murdered. Someone is burning buildings which are owned by Mrs. Arkbari. Whoever killed the women was connected to the buildings and Mrs. Arkbari. My guess is Mrs. A knows who killed the young women. But it wasn't her.

The arsonist is upset about the murders. Just guessing, but the arsonist knew there might be more bodies. The arsonist has a personal interest in finding the killer.

I thought only Phil had the means to do the arson, that only he had access to the Avgas, but it's more readily available than it should be. So anyone could have had the means. So then, the question is who had the motive?

Let's put aside her notices on NextDoor complaining about her neighbor's dog pooping on the front lawn as a motive. Let's put aside the fact that she's a horrible woman in general as a motive. Also, I don't believe this is based on some internet Facebook feud because of something she wrote about Israel and the Gaza Strip. Many, many people put many things on social media and no one tries to burn down their businesses or possessions. This is something personal. The person who is burning these places is in some way tied to the murdered women. But we don't know who the murdered women are.

Do you Have a Mother or a Motive?

I wanted to rule out one idea. So I called Phil. "Hi, Phil."

"Good afternoon, sunshine. How can I help you?"

"I'm coming into the office to talk to the guys as they wrap up for the day and I was hoping you'd be there too."

"Absolutely. I'm coming back to the office now to work on paperwork. It would be nice to see you."

"It would be nice to see you too. I had a horrible weekend with my family."

"I get it," he said. "I flew home to help. My mom had me clean out her garage last month, and yet I'm still the ungrateful son who never helps."

Phil helped his mom—that was good to know.

"I'm just glad I don't have any siblings," I said, "or my mom would be busy comparing me to them. My girlfriend is one of three kids and she's the only one not married and her mom is always telling her, Well, you know, you should really get someone in your life like your sister.'"

"Oh," Phil laughed, "I'm one of four kids and my mom decided early on that my oldest sister was the golden child, so me and my two brothers don't bother competing."

So Phil had a living sister and a mother. Because my theory at this point was that the women murdered were special to the arsonist—either their mom or their sister, or someone close. Ok, I could be wrong. It could be their girlfriend, or their aunt, or their... But Phil was sounding normal and I wanted him to be innocent, and I wanted to go to dinner with him, and I wanted this damn case to end.

I wanted the sky to open, the sun to shine and the arsonist and killer to both be illuminated by God with a big shining ray. Seemed like the best chance right now to work out who was guilty. So I gave a silent prayer and promised to sacrifice a chicken to whatever god made this clear.

"Well, I'll see you at the office then," I said.

"Yep, see you here."

It was time to talk to Harry, for in his intermittent grunts I could often find clarity.

"Yep," he answered in Harry fashion.

"I've got any idea. Can you find out from your friends in the LAPD if there are any cold cases from about twenty years ago in the LA Hollywood area? The victim would have been a woman in her twenties and she would have been killed by a blow to the back of the head."

"You have an idea," said Harry.

"Yes."

"Ok. It might take a while."

"Thanks, Harry. Call me if you find anything."

I pulled into the parking lot of Bronson Construction's office glad I hadn't had so much time on my hands that I'd been forced to call my mother rather than listen to the voices in my head.

It was possible that I knew what the motive was. Now I just needed to work out who had that motive.

I parked the car and walked into the office. Amanda was, as always, sitting at her desk leaning forward slightly to see the screen but not wearing reading glasses that might have made it a little easier.

She turned, squinting at me. "Mario's on his way in with Armando. They'll be here in five minutes. Do you want to sit over there," she pointed at the conference table, "or drag everyone out to the park bench again?"

Got to love it that she was criticizing my methods before she'd even said hi. "I will play it by ear," I answered. "Francisco isn't in the office this afternoon?" I said, pointing to her boss's empty desk.

"He's only usually here for the weekly meetings. Apart from that, he's at the jobsites and it's just me."

"I suppose it gets a little lonely."

"Oh, I can't get anything done when they are here. It's better when they are all gone."

I wondered if she wanted everyone gone: all her coworkers, her family, humans on planet Earth. And yet I was sure she was neither my arsonist nor my killer.

Armando and Mario came into the office looking at me.

"She wants to talk to you," said Amanda with all the grace and tact she thought I deserved.

I decided to talk to Mario first. He seemed the least likely candidate and this should be easy.

"Mario, I just had a couple more questions for you if you don't mind taking a walk with me." I gave Amanda a side eye as I passed in front of her desk for the freedom of the outdoors. "I'm just trying to close up the case and I had a couple of questions. Of course, you need to know that I will be able to double-check your answers, so you might as well answer honestly the first time."

I'd decided to go at Mario directly. He was younger than me, and struck me as a boy who took orders from everyone, even if he didn't always obey them. He nodded so I started.

"Has anyone in your family or friends ever been murdered?"

"Oh yeah. My cousin Julian. He was shot in a gang thing. I mean, we wasn't in the gang but you know, he was there so, you know... My aunt was so upset, and then later, when my cousin Tony went to jail, she was kind of left with no kids if you know what I mean, so I had to be, you know, her kid and stuff. But my own mother, God bless her soul, says my aunt needs me more than she does. So I eat dinner there, ya know."

"Do you have any sisters, Mario?"

"Oh yeah, two. They are younger than me, but they still don't listen to anything I say."

"Have you heard about the bodies they've found downtown in the two buildings that burned?"

"Nope. Someone got caught in a fire, huh? Well, that's too bad."

"Yes, it is." I was walking him back to the office. There was just no way he was involved. I mentally checked him off my list and smiled. "Thanks for talking to me, Mario. Have a safe drive home."

I walked into the office. Armando was still putting away tools in the backroom. I followed him back there. He looked tired, bent up over the toolbox, trying to take everything out for the night.

"Armando, can I ask you a few questions?"

"Ok."

"Do you have a reason to hate Mrs. Arkbari?"

I thought I saw the corner of his mouth turn up a little. "Hate is a hard word."

"Has anyone in your family ever been murdered?"

"Sure," he said. "My wife was murdered when my kids was little."

"Oh my God. What happened?"

"She was on her way home from work and she was mugged. At least that's what they thought first."

"Mugged?"

"She was working late all the time and I was home with the baby." His eyes were suddenly clearer, and he was a young man re-experiencing the death of his wife again. "Anyway, it was a long time ago." He put the last of the tools on the shelf.

"I'm so sorry."

"Thanks. Anyway, what was your question?"

"Just wondering if you'd heard about the bodies they've found in the warehouse downtown."

"Heard it on the news. Three dead, not sure if they died in the fire or not. Doesn't make sense, so many dead people in the same area."

He was right, it was the same area. Why hadn't I thought of that?

"Thanks, Armando. By the way, where do you live?"

"Pacoima."

"Near the Whiteman Airfield?"

"Sort of. I can hear the planes all night long."

Armando had just put himself as prime suspect number one. And it made me sad. I didn't want to push more. Let me talk to everyone else and hear what Harry found out. I was working off the assumption that someone had lost a twenty-year-old relative about twenty years ago, but I could be barking up the wrong construction worker's leg.

I let Armando and Mario go home, and Peet and Steve arrived. I figured I'd start with Steve.

I decided to do the sit down on the park bench across from my suspect and do the adversarial stare across the table. Like a bad first date at IHoP. "So, Steve, where were you last night?"

"With my girlfriend at the Green Day concert." He held up his phone. He'd been up front near the mosh pit. "It was awesome."

"Oh wow," I said, leaning over to hear the badly recorded music on the shaky video he'd taken with his phone. "That would have been amazing! They were playing at SoFi, right?"

"Yep."

"I hate that venue," I said with more passion than I usually feel for anything apart from bad Starbucks holiday drinks.

"It took us two hours to drive out, we paid eighty dollars for parking, and then they didn't open all the entrances and we all had to file out the same way. Green Day were great but I am never going to SoFi again. My girlfriend bought the tickets so I don't know what they cost but would have been better anywhere else. I lined up for an hour for food and then they didn't want to let me back down to the floor. Almost had to hit someone."

Well, whatever else Steve was, he definitely wasn't an arsonist out torching a warehouse yesterday.

"So sorry," I answered. "Have any of the other guys talked about relatives being murdered?"

"Armando and Peet. Both their wives got killed. They met at some support group, and Armando got Peet his job here. I guess the neighborhoods they lived in were pretty rough. Peet said they thought he did it, but he didn't, and that he misses her every day."

"Thanks, Steve. Head on back to the office. I'll be there in a minute."

I pulled up my phone for Peet's credit report. How had I missed it? I may not be able to take his fingerprints and check his police report but his credit report was accessible. Peet didn't have any credit more than two years old. This didn't make a lot of sense for a man in his 40s. Unless he was using a different name two years ago. Or unless he wasn't able to get credit.

I went into the office and Amanda snarled at me. "You know I need to leave the office by 5 p.m."

"All the guys aren't back yet," I responded.

"That's not the point. They have keys. You don't have a key. I can't stay for you."

"You can go, Amanda. I will lock up," Phil said walking up behind me. I turned to him and smiled.

"Nice to see you."

"Sure, whatever you say, Phil," simpered Amanda with a small flirty smile for Phil.

God I hate women who treat men differently than they treat women. I mean, misogynistic males are the least of our problems when there are so many misogynistic females.

Peet walked in behind Phil. It was time to talk to Peet, and I couldn't put it off. I decided to corner him in the back tool room where he was still putting things away. "Hey, Peet, can you talk with me?"

"If God so wills it," said Peet with a resigned look on his face.

I shut the door to the tool room behind us. It was a small room with workbenches on three walls and tools stored on shelves covering the fourth wall. There was nowhere to run. He was trapped with me. I hoped I hadn't made a huge mistake. I turned to him and said, "I know what you did."

He put his tool kit down on the wooden workbench and looked down at it, his back to me. "I didn't do anything."

"Your wife was killed. Someone hit her on the back of the head. You were sent away for the murder."

"Yes, but I didn't do anything." He turned slowly to me, his face twisted in pain. "I loved her so much. She was pregnant with our baby, and I didn't even know."

I pointed to a chair in the corner of the tool room and he walked over. His hopping had turned to a shuffle.

"Tell me about your wife. Tell me what happened.""She worked for Mrs. Arkbari and her brother's business, and she was on her way home. The office was downtown then, near Chinatown.""I was still standing and he looked up at me. His voice started to catch in his throat as he spoke. "She'd left work and was on her way to the train station and she was killed in an alleyway. Someone heard a noise and saw a figure running away leaving her lying there face down. The police decided it was me."

He looked down at his feet, his arms limp by his side. "I wasn't a great guy then, but I loved her."

"What was her name?"

"Michelle. She had skin like fine velvet and when she'd get mad at me her nose would wrinkle up. We'd only been married a year. And we fought a lot. About money, about her job. She wanted a kid and I didn't think we could afford one."

"People heard your fights?" I said, crouching down to look him in the eyes.

"Yeah, we was loud. At the trial all these people said I had hurt her, but I never touched her, never hurt her like that."

"So you went away for it?"

He nodded. "LAPD wanted to make sure they were solving cases. Murder rates had climbed and the new police chief wanted to keep his job, so they had to do something."

"Why do you think Mrs. Arkbari murdered her?"

"That was where my Michelle worked. She was leaving work when it happened. Mrs. Arkbari got on the stand and said my Michelle was a bad woman."

"What did she say?"

He lifted his head to look me straight in the face. "She said that Michelle was meeting a boyfriend after work. She said I probably wasn't the father of the baby. She said Michelle was going to leave me..." He started to cry.

"When did you get out of prison?"

"Three years ago." He rubbed his eyes and his nose on his t-shirt.

"But you didn't start burning her places till now."

"It was hard to find a job. And I was trying to put it behind me. Then she came to our worksite, to that apartment." He rubbed the back of his hand across his nose and sniffed. "She had no heart. Those people were losing their home."

"And you got mad."

"Yeah, but I was real careful not to hurt anyone."

"You were just trying to hurt her."

"Yep, and I was just going down the list of the buildings she owned."

"The list on the outside of Amanda's file box?" I said, realizing that I'd seen this list so many times without taking note of it. Of course! The buildings had been burned in the order Amanda filed them. Why hadn't I seen that? Why hadn't I thought of that? "You didn't think she was a murderer when you started?"

"No, but then when the cigarette shop had a dead woman..."

Now that his story was pouring out of his mouth his eyes couldn't stop pouring either. He rubbed his arm against his face. "When I heard that the poor woman in the cigarette shop was hit on the back of the head... She was killed the same way as my Michelle."

"I have to report you to the police."

He put his head down. "As God wills."

He was limp, collapsed in the chair. I opened the door and walked back out into the main office. It was obvious that everyone had been listening. Amanda and Phil were right by the entrance to the tool room. "Phil, can you make sure Peet doesn't go anywhere? Amanda, please call 911 and ask for the police." I picked up my phone and texted Harry.

"Harry, I have the arsonist. He's not the murderer."

I then locked the front door to the office. If Peet made a run for it, that would slow him down. Amanda pushed the desk phone at me. "I don't know what to say."

Which of course, she didn't. So I explained it to the 911 operator and they said they would dispatch police. I grabbed the tissues off Amanda's desk and went back to the tool room where Peet was still sitting with Phil standing in front of him.

"Here," I said, handing him the tissues.

He took one and blew his nose. "I loved her, you know."

"Yeah."

He dried his eyes but they continued to leak. "Mrs. Arkbari killed all these women."

"I don't think it was her, Peet."

"Somebody did it. Somebody killed Michelle, and those other women too. How many other bodies are there?" he asked, looking straight at me. "I only burned four buildings and there are four women who died already. How many more?"

How many more was a question I'd been asking for a while.

My phone rang. It was Detective Longe.

"Harry just called me. He said you have the arsonist."

"Yep, and we led 911 to get some beat cops to pick him up."

"Ok. I'm in the area. Send me your location."

"I can hear the sirens already," I said. "Where do you want them to take him to?"

"Downtown. I'll meet them there."

"Ok," I said and hung up as the police charged into the parking lot like kids sliding into high school assembly as the bell rang.

I unlocked the door and went out before they came in guns blazing.

I want to die one day but not because I was caught in a blaze of bullets shot off by overexcited cops. I walked out hands down and open. "I called you," I yelled. "The suspect is in the office. He's not armed, or resisting. Detective Longe is going to meet you downtown."

"Ok," said the oldest policeman, looking at his partner and the four other policemen who had also arrived in two other cars.

Peet came limping out of the office, his arms in the air. They pushed him down against the car hood with more force than necessary and cuffed him. The two extra cars left and he got into the back seat of the patrol car slowly. "I just wanted justice," he said to me as they closed the door.

I wanted justice too.

When the End is Less Satisfying than the Beginning

I called Harry. "You got my text?"

"Yep."

"Can you get Mrs. Arkbari to meet us at her office?"

"Yep."

"Ok, I am on my way there."

The drive to Mrs. Arkbari's office seemed longer than it had any other time this week. I'd done what I was hired to do and instead of feeling satisfied I was sad. I'd found the criminal, and he was also the victim. And yet the real crimes were still unsolved.

There were at least four murders. The man who had gone away for the murder of his pregnant wife was not the killer. Peet was just another victim. He wasn't the killer, so someone else was. And Mrs. A knew who had done it. Of this I was sure.

Harry arrived at the same time I did, which meant he must have driven like a bat out of hell. Mrs. Arkbari was also pulling up but since she'd come three miles that was hardly a challenge.

Harry walked to her car and opened the door for her, helping her out. Like the gentleman he had never ever been.

She was walking with a stick today and leaned against him slightly for support. I opened the door and he sat her down while Maria looked up, surprised. She hadn't known we were coming in.

"Can I get everyone a cup of tea or coffee?" asked Maria.

Harry reached into his pocket, pulled out a wad of bills in a money clip (ones on the outside, like a gentleman) and peeled off two twenties from the inside. "Can you go to Starbucks and get us all a drink?"

Maria looked to Mrs. Arkbari, who nodded. "What would you like, Mrs. Arkbari?"

"Black coffee with a shot of espresso."

"Same for me," said Harry, "But add some sugar."

"And I'll have a triple-shot latte large," I said.

Maria nodded and went and picked up her purse. She turned with a puzzled expression at me before she walked out, closing the door.

"We found the arsonist, Mrs. Arkbari," said Harry.

"Oh, you did," she said, lowering herself into her seat.

"Yes. The police took him into custody," I said. "You know him. You testified against him and got him arrested for murdering his wife."

"Peet..." she said, the name coming to her instantly. She looked up at me in recognition and pulled her lips thin between her teeth. "He's the one who burned my buildings." It wasn't a question. It all made sense now.

"But you knew he wasn't the murderer even then, didn't you?"

"I didn't know. I didn't know for sure. I mean, I was sorry Michelle was dead, and I thought he'd probably done it. They fought a lot."

"What was Michelle's job?"

"She was my brother Aaron's secretary." The faintest look of dis-taste passed Mrs. A's face. She was too accustomed to being questioned to break, at least not easily.

"What happened?"

"I didn't see it."

"What happened?"

"Someone hit her in the back of her head, breaking her skull, on her way home, in the alleyway near our office."

"And you knew it wasn't Peet."

"I don't know what I knew." She looked down at her feet, her mouth tight.

"But when the first body was found in the smoke shop—you knew then. You knew all of it then."

"Yes," she said, looking up, her eyes completely dry. "I knew then."

"What did you know?" said Harry, walking up to lean on the desk next to me. He'd instantly become part of the gang playing the good cop.

"I knew Aaron had killed Michelle, and Penelope."

"Who's Penelope?" I asked.

"His wife. I mean, we thought she fell down the stairs but when Michelle died I wasn't sure, because they both had the same injuries."

"And then the body in the cigarette shop," said Harry quietly. "You knew then. Did you know there would be more bodies in the warehouse?"

"No," she said, lifting her head higher and pursing her lips tighter. "I didn't know there would be more. How could I? How could I think that my baby brother, the boy I carried around when he was hurt, the boy I watched grow could be doing this? Killing not one person or two, but I don't know how many. I don't know."

She was as close to crying as she was capable.

"You knew," I said. "You just didn't want to know."

"Perhaps, perhaps."

Conversations with the Dying

Maria came back with the drinks and we grabbed them and walked out to Mrs. Arkbari's car. She was going to drive. To take us to meet this monster. We drove in silence. I was in the backseat and I texted Detective Longe the information we had so far and our destination. He said he'd meet us there. Which made sense. This was going to be a huge scoop for him. I'd just solved a serial killer mystery no one knew had happened, and now it was time to confront the murderer.

I didn't know how to feel, and I think the feeling was mutual. The car was filled with a quiet void, and only the air conditioning made noise until we arrived at the memory care facility where Aaron was already a prisoner.

We walked in and Detective Longe was already there. "I tried to get in to see him and they said I needed a family member to let me in or a warrant."

Mrs. Arkbari nodded at the woman behind the desk. "They are all with me." She turned to us. "You will have to sign in."

Detective Longe muttered under his breath, "It would be easier to break into a prison."

He wasn't wrong.

"Can you have him brought to the courtyard?" asked Mrs. Arkbari.

"Sure," said the woman at the desk, and started making calls.

We followed Mrs. Arkbari through the facility. It was better than anything I'd ever seen before. This was not the budget, all-my-family-could-afford facility that my grandmother had ended up in. This was what money could buy. Beauty and the illusion of freedom. It was set up like a modern apartment building with lots of windows and doors that opened up into a central courtyard garden.

The courtyard was beautifully landscaped, with small ponds with fish and a fountain. It was large and open, and above the sky showed another lovely Los Angeles day in the mid-eighties. We sat under an umbrella on upholstered wicker outdoor furniture.

It didn't take long until we saw an old man being rolled in a wheelchair towards us.

They pushed him in the shade next to his sister.

"Hello, Aaron," she said, and he said nothing. Sitting still and quiet like someone not awake.

"What's wrong with him?" asked Detective Longe, who was still a couple miles behind the starting gate.

"He has Alzheimer's," said Mrs. Arkbari. "It's been five years since he was diagnosed."

"Oh," said Longe, realizing that he wasn't going to get a glorious arrest.

This man was never going to prison. He was already imprisoned in his own mind and body. I was just hoping he'd be able to talk a little. Tell us something.

"Does he talk?" asked Longe.

"Sometimes," Mrs. Arkbari answered. "Just less."

I looked over at Mrs. Arkbari, and at her hair. It would have been long and dark when she was young. I pulled my hair out of the scrunchy I'd tied it into when I'd gotten up. I was hoping it would work.

"I want to try something," I said, looking at Mrs. Arkbari. She nodded.

I turned his wheelchair towards me so the only person he could see was me and I leaned down and spoke directly into his hearing aid. "Hello, Aaron. It's me."

"Penelope," he said, reaching for my face. "Why, Penelope?"

I had thought that he would think I was his sister, not his dead wife, but at least he was talking. "I loved you," I said.

"You were going to leave me. Everyone was going to leave me."

"How many women did you kill, Aaron?"

"They were going to leave me. They were all going to leave me."

"How many, Aaron?"

"I hid them all so good. You won't find them."

"How many, Aaron? Me, and Michelle, and the girl at the shop on 4th Street, and the three at your dad's warehouse…"

"How did you know about them, Penelope? I didn't tell anybody."

"I know everything, Aaron. How many more did you kill? How many more after me?"

"Just ten. Only ten."

"So me, then ten more, Aaron?"

"None of them loved me, Penelope. I just wanted them to love me."

"Where are the other bodies, Aaron?"

"Oh, I was so clever. Whenever we were remodeling a building I'd hide one. But I was worried about the smell, you know. So first I would put them in salt. I had a big salt barrel, then when they were dry I'd put them in the building. Dad never knew.""So you kept it a secret.""Oh yes. Nobody knew. I think maybe Rose was suspicious." He looked over at Mrs. Arkbari and for a moment he was looking at his baby sister Rose.

Then the spell was over. He turned suddenly and looked at the sky. "The sky is blue today."

"Yes," I said. "It is blue."

"Do I know you?" he asked.

"No," I answered.

He smiled and stared at the sky, his neck bobbing about. Then he went still, focused on an invisible point only he could see.

I stood up and started to cry. Harry put his arms around me and held me to his chest. "You did good, kid. We'll find the rest of the bodies, and the families can have some peace."

I started to sob harder. Harry held me tighter.

Detective Longe started to talk to the nurse. "Is there any chance Aaron could tell us more?"

"Doubt it. Those are the most words I've heard in a year," said the young man. "Maybe right before the end. Sometimes they get real lucid right before the end."

The detective nodded at me and went back to Mrs. Arkbari. "I am expecting your full cooperation in helping to locate the rest of the victims," he said with a veiled threat in his voice.

"Of course," she said.

"We will leave separately," said Harry, and he left the detective and the old lady in the beautiful garden made for the dying.

"Kid, I hope you got one of those Uber apps because I'm taking you to eat and you are going to celebrate with a hot fudge sundae."

I smiled at him.

"You know, kid, you just solved ten cold cases. Not too bad."

"I guess so." And my brain bounced out of the reality of the ugly I had just uncovered and I thought Phil isn't a suspect anymore so I also might have a date for Saturday.

"You done good, kid, real good."

"Some families will have peace."

"And you will have chocolate syrup."

He was right. I deserved a damn sundae.

Also by Anne Shelley

SOILED DOVES

Tombstone, Arizona 1881. The last gasp of the wild west.

Lily's husband brought her to the frontier in search of a better life. But his sudden death leaves her penniless and far from anyone who might help her.

Desperate to survive and out of respectable options, Lily crosses a line she fears can never be uncrossed: the brothel door.

As a soiled dove Lily finds fascinating new friends and a sense of community she never imagined. But when the women are threatened, is there anything they won't do to protect each other?

SOPHIE DRAKE AND THE DROWNING MAN

Where's the missing millionaire, will Sophie find him or has he already drowned in the lake?

Before she became a PI Sophie Drake was a peace officer in a quiet tourist town. Until the quiet was shattered by an empty fishing boat and a missing millionaire.

SOPHIE DRAKE AND THE TRAIL OF LIES
Somewhere in Las Vegas, two Women have disappeared. Sin City keeps its secrets hidden, but maybe not from the people living beneath its streets.

At five foot two Sophie Drake is used to being underestimated, but even she doesn't think she can solve this case. An heiress has been kidnapped and her assistant Emily is missing.
The FBI think Emily was involved in the kidnapping but Sophie thinks she is innocent and possibly dead. Can Sophie untangle the lies and find Emily before it's too late?

SOPHIE DRAKE AND THE CRUISE TO HELL (COMING SOON)
Sophie has been dragged on a cruise with Harry, his mother Lilibeth and his girlfriend Rosie. She thinks the hardest thing is going to be keeping Lilibeth from overeating at the buffet.
Until Sophia finds Lilibeth's new friend Violet dead on the top deck of the ship. Lilibeth is sure that Violet was murdered. The ship doctor is sure she died of a an accidental medication overdose.
But does that explain the near death of the man in the cabin next to Violet's?

Preview of: Sophie Drake and the Cruise to Hell

CHAPTER 1: IN THE SHADOW OF THE REAPER

L ife is hard. It's a performance art. As anyone who's ever watched a child on a piece of equipment in the park knows, it's relatively easy to climb to the top of the slide. You think it's difficult on the way up, but then you are there. And all the stress and trials it took to get there look insignificant from the top of the climb. Then you have to find the courage to go down again. But if you really want the maximum amount of pain and discomfort, all you really need to do is tank the dismount.

I remember watching gymnastics when I was a kid. I watched this gymnast do beautiful flips and soar through the air like an angel, and everything was going right, and then she'd overthought it and tried too hard. She landed after twisting slightly, shattering her thigh bone and lying on the floor, crying like a baby.

Children have similar issues going down the slide. Everything's right till you get to almost the bottom and then you lean back. And whack the back of your head on the sharp edge of the slide as you shoot off the end onto the sand.

Getting old is much like this. You've been going through just fine. Cruising through your emotions and experiences. You think you've worked it out. Looks like everything's good, then all of a sudden you find yourself at the top of the slide with only one way out. And the only question is, is it going to be a long, slow ride done with grace and style, or a short one?

Some of this is your choice. Perhaps you are the person who decides to go face-first, screaming all the way down. Or maybe it's going to be one of those long, slow, painful, drawn-out processes where you're lying on your back, knocking your head from side to side until eventually, when you finally get to the dismount, there's nothing left of you but a broken shell of your former self.

Harry's mom Lilibeth was definitely on that slide. How close to the bottom she was was anybody's guess. If you'd asked her, she was going to live 'til she was a hundred and twenty. Which, since she'd been saying that since eighty and she was now pretty close to a hundred, so it may actually be correct. Personally, I was hoping that when my time came, I wouldn't reach the slide until I was ready to go. Then take the short slide. And check-out quickly, shooting off the end into nothing without biting through my lip or pissing myself on the way out.

Mrs. Violet Young's slide was over and she'd been dead on the twelfth floor sundeck overlooking the pool, in a pink athleisure suit and new Mexican sombrero, for at least half an hour before anyone noticed.

I was silly enough to find the body.

COMING FALL 2025